SCHROEDER'S GAME

SCHROEDER'S GAME

by

ARTHUR MALING

LONDON
VICTOR GOLLANCZ LTD
1977

01010272

Printed in Great Britain by
Lowe & Brydone Printers Limited, Thetford, Norfolk

-1-

If a crisis has to occur, I'd just as soon it wouldn't occur on a Monday morning. For that's when I hold my weekly staff meeting and when I'm least ready to cope with anything else.

But this crisis did occur on a Monday morning. And it shook the hell out of me.

The meeting was in progress. It had developed into an exceptionally lively one. My staff consists of five people. Since the six of us usually work independently, spending a lot of time on the road, the only chance we have to get together as a group and compare notes is at the beginning of the week, before we scatter. The information and opinions we exchange then form the basis of the market letter which we send to our customers every Tuesday and which our customers seem to regard as one of the most valuable services our company provides.

As always, the meeting began with a discussion of the market's performance during the past week. On this particular Monday that didn't take long, because the market hadn't done much. The Dow-Jones industrials had dribbled along, closing on Friday a mere three points above where they'd opened on the preceding Monday. Our collective view was that they'd continue to dribble along for another couple of weeks, until the President delivered his State of the Union address.

Then the interesting stuff began to come out.

Harriet Jensen had heard a rumor that the Citizens Bank of Northern California was seriously overextended.

Joe Rothland had been told that the Justice Department was preparing an antitrust suit against Federated Office Equipment.

Irving Silvers, on a trip to Detroit, had learned that automobile sales were going to exceed the estimates that the Big Three had privately made.

George Cole was looking into a report that the president of Valueland Food Stores had met secretly in Palm Springs with the owner of the King drug chain to discuss merger.

And Brian Barth, the freshman member of my team, had picked up his first important item: the news that Kenwood Oil Company was about to form a subsidiary to manufacture jackup rigs for offshore drilling; it would use some of the rigs itself and lease others to anyone who wanted them.

What pleased me was not so much that Brian had acquired the information, but that he was handling himself well under attack. For Irving had challenged him and was giving him a hard time. Irving is my right-hand man and the one who's in charge of the others when I'm not around. Although he's fiercely loyal to me, he's also protective of them. Occasionally, however, he gets a bit rough with one of them, and he was being especially rough with Brian. It was his way of teaching the kid.

Which is what Brian was: a kid. I'd hired him away from the firm that does our accounting. He was only twenty-six years old, a plump, baby-faced Virginian with blue eyes, pink cheeks and a deferential manner. I doubted that he had to shave oftener than once a week. But behind the façade of immaturity lurked one of the toughest, brightest, most determined spirits I'd ever encountered. Brian Barth was no one to tangle with. He could, without losing his cool or his air of humility, make you feel like an utter fool. As Irving was finding out.

I was sitting there listening to the two of them go at it. I figured that I'd give them a few more minutes, then intervene by changing the subject.

2

But suddenly my telephone rang.

I frowned at it. Helen Doyle, my secretary, knew that I didn't want to be disturbed.

It rang again.

I picked it up. "Yes," I snapped.

"Mr. Petacque would like to see you in his office," Helen said. Tom Petacque is one of my two partners.

"Tell Mr. Petacque I'll see him later." I put the telephone down sharply and turned to Brian. "You were saying . . ."

"I was saying, sir, that the Indonesian government—"

"Indonesian government!" Irving exclaimed. "The subsidiary hasn't even been formed yet, and already you've got it dealing with foreign governments!"

"Well, sir," Brian replied evenly, "wouldn't you say that before investing the kind of money that Kenwood will have to invest, they'd make sure they had some customers lined up?"

"I would not! I'd say that they'd *like* to have some customers lined up. And the government of Indonesia—"

Once more the telephone rang.

"Damn," I said. I put the telephone to my face. "I do not want to be disturbed," I said very distinctly. "I thought I made that clear."

It was Mark Price, my other partner. "You get your fucking ass into Tom's office this minute!" he shouted, and hung up.

I was thunderstruck. Mark isn't the easiest person in the world to like, but whatever his faults, he's not coarse. He rarely swears, and in all the years I'd known him I'd never heard him use the words "fucking" or "ass." And I'd never heard him as angry as he'd sounded just then.

I put the telephone down and got to my feet. "Excuse me, people," I said. "I'll be back in a minute." I hurried out of my office and down the corridor to Tom's.

Even if Mark hadn't spoken as he had, I'd have known, the moment I entered the room, that something was radically wrong. By the way the two of them looked. Mark was standing beside the

3

desk, glowering and so rigid that he seemed scarcely human. Tom was slumped in the desk chair, his face the color of ashes, his jaw muscles working furiously, his eyes fixed on the floor. "What's the matter?" I asked.

Still rigid, Mark said, "Shut the door, and listen to what this fucking idiot wants to do."

I closed the door and went across to the desk. I said nothing. I merely waited.

"Go ahead," Mark said to Tom. "Tell him."

Tom raised his eyes. There was anguish in them. "I've decided to sell my interest in the business," he said. "You and Mark have first option. Do you want it?"

I gripped the edge of the desk. It was, at that instant, the only reality I could find. "You can't do that," I said. My voice had suddenly gone hoarse.

"If you don't want it," Tom continued as if he hadn't heard me, "I have another buyer. The price to you two is three-quarters of a million, although I can get more from him. Will you take it?"

I glanced at Mark. He was beginning to relax. Sharing the news with me seemed to have eased the strain on him. He met my gaze but didn't speak.

"You have forty-eight hours to make up your minds," Tom said, and lapsed into his former posture, staring at the floor.

I cleared my throat. "Mark's right. You're a fucking idiot."

Tom didn't reply.

I walked over to the couch and sat down. I felt as if I'd been punched in the stomach. Tom, Mark and I were quite different from one another in temperament, and we'd often disagreed. Occasionally, after a spat, one of us would walk around for a day or two with his nose out of joint. But never in the five years we'd been in business together had we had anything even approaching a serious quarrel. And beneath whatever surface friction existed there was a solid layer of mutual trust, admiration and respect.

Furthermore, when we'd parted on Friday afternoon there'd

4

been no hint of an impending storm. Tom had been jovial and optimistic.

And finally, the price was too low. It was true that according to the bylaws, if one of us decided to sell his interest in the business he had to offer it to the other two before he could offer it to anyone else. But the bylaws didn't specify the price, and three-quarters of a million was ridiculous. Therefore, no other buyer was waiting in the wings. Tom had simply made up his mind to get out and was trying to force Mark and me into letting him do so.

Yet the fact that there was no other buyer at the moment didn't mean that Tom wouldn't find one in the near future, especially if he was willing to sell cheap.

The whole thing seemed somehow phony. However, there was nothing phony about Tom's expression. Stress was written all over his face.

An anxiety attack, I decided. He'd had one once before. He'd been hospitalized with it.

"Let's all simmer down," I said, "and discuss this thing objectively. Business is good, Tom. We've just finished the best year we've ever had. And there's no reason to believe that this year won't be even better. If I've offended you in any way, I'm sorry. If Mark has offended you in any way, I'm sure he's sorry too. We don't want anyone sitting in that chair but you, so we're not going to buy you out and we're not going to let you sell to anyone else either."

Tom stood up. I could see, even from where I was sitting, that he was trembling. "You can't stop me."

"We can make it difficult for you, though," Mark said. Then he relented. He went around the desk and put his hand on Tom's arm. And since Mark seldom displays affection, I realized that he too was deeply moved. "Please, Tom," he said gently, "sit down and be reasonable. I didn't mean to lose my temper."

Tom shook the hand off. "Don't try to humor me—either of

you. I've made up my mind, and that's all there is to it. I'm selling. You have forty-eight hours. Think it over." He went to the closet, put on his overcoat and without looking at Mark or me, walked stiffly out of the office.

After a moment Mark came over to the couch and sat down. "I'm appalled," he said, reverting to the kind of language that was characteristic of him. He often sounded like the late President Franklin Roosevelt, which was understandable, for while they were two generations apart, they'd had the same sort of education. "Utterly appalled."

"There's no other buyer," I said.

"I'm inclined to agree with you." He frowned, then added, "I'm afraid he's having another breakdown."

I gave him a startled glance. Tom's breakdown had occurred ten years before, shortly after I met him. Neither of us had been acquainted with Mark at that time. I had no idea that Mark knew about it.

Evidently he guessed what I was thinking. "Tom told me," he said. "When we were talking about forming the company. He said he felt obliged to, in case it might influence me."

"I'm glad he did," was all I could say.

"What he needs is a rest, a change of scene. Perhaps some professional help. If my poor mother . . ." He paused. He'd once told me, in a moment of intimacy, that his mother had been an alcoholic. His father had refused to let her go to a psychiatrist. With the result that in a drunken haze she'd accidentally fallen down a flight of steps and been killed. "A good doctor is what he needs."

"I think you're right. But damn it, Mark, nervous breakdowns don't come on all of a sudden. I'm no expert on the subject, but I know that much. There are symptoms, then more symptoms. It's not like appendicitis. And just three days ago Tom was on top of the world."

"That's true."

"I simply don't understand it."

6

"Neither do I. But I think you'd better have a talk with him. You're closer to him than I am. Go to his house. Try to get through to him."

I'd already half made up my mind to do just that. "I will."

Through the closed door I heard the telephone ring in the office of Tom's secretary.

Mark brushed a piece of lint from the leg of his pants. I looked at Tom's unoccupied desk. I wondered what I'd say to him when I did go to his house.

"I guess there's nothing else we can do at the moment," Mark said, getting up.

"I guess not." I got up too. "I'd better go back to my meeting."

We walked out of Tom's office together.

"Do either of you know," Tom's secretary asked as we passed her desk, "when Mr. Petacque will be back? He didn't say."

"No," Mark replied with a sigh. "But I'm afraid he's liable to be gone for quite a while."

–2–

When the others filed out after the meeting, Irving stayed behind.

"Is anything wrong, Brock?"

I shook my head. Usually I confided in him, but this was one problem that I felt should be kept between Mark, Tom and myself. "No, Irving."

He eyed me owlishly. "Well, if there's anything I can do."

"No. Nothing. You were a little rough on Brian, though, I thought."

He grinned. "That kid's terrific. But I have a hunch he'll be after my job in another couple of months."

I managed to grin also. "Another couple of months? He's after it already."

"Maybe I ought to start reading the want ads?"

"Maybe. But not on company time."

He laughed and started for the door. Then he came back. His expression was serious again. "Really, if there's anything I can do, Brock . . ."

I put my arm on his shoulder. "As a matter of fact, Irving, there is. You can go to lunch."

"O.K. O.K." He left.

I paced the floor for a few minutes, then decided to go to lunch myself. I wasn't hungry, but I thought it would be a good idea to get out of the office for a while.

I chose a restaurant that none of us ever went to, for I didn't want to meet anyone. I wanted to sit alone and sort out my thoughts.

I tried to be honest with myself, to see things as they really were.

I was fonder of Tom than I was of Mark. But I had more confidence in Mark than I had in Tom.

Both of them were fonder of me than they were of each other. Both of them had more confidence in me than they had in each other.

I was the balance wheel. Had been from the beginning.

But whatever our inner feelings, the three of us were a good combination. The abilities of one complemented the abilities of the others.

And in a way I needed both of them more than they needed me. Not only for business reasons. For emotional reasons. Each of them had a family; I didn't. *They* were my family.

Price, Potter and Petacque could survive without Tom. So could I. But the company wouldn't be the same, and neither would I.

Tom couldn't be allowed to sell out.

Tom didn't actually want to sell out.

I finished my first martini and ordered another. Over the second I excluded Mark from my thoughts and zoomed in on Tom.

He was one of the first friends I made after moving to New York. We worked for the same brokerage house. Both of us were new there. Tom was in sales. I was in research. He'd recently married. Daisy, his wife, and I hit it off. The three of us spent a lot of time together. When their son was born, they made me his godfather.

As time passed, Tom and I did well. But we wanted to do even better and we felt stymied. We began to talk of starting a brokerage house of our own. One that would deal not with the general public but only with big purchasers, like mutual funds and banks. Between us we had a fair amount of money, though not enough. Then we met Mark. He'd pulled out of his father's business, had more money than he knew what to do with, owned a seat on the New York Stock Exchange and was trading for his own account. He liked the idea of starting a specialty house of the sort we had in mind. Thus Price, Potter and Petacque came into being. The three of us were equal partners. Mark was in charge of the office and the financing, Tom was in charge of sales, and I ran the research department. And at a time when most brokerage houses were doing badly, ours was successful. Some of the biggest funds in existence liked our service and gave us large chunks of their business.

None of us could have done it alone, but as a team we clicked. And Tom's contribution was enormous.

On the surface, I mused, over the second martini, Tom had more going for him than any man I knew. He was good-looking, charming, physically adept, witty, generous, kind. People of all sorts were drawn to him. He always tried to do the right thing and usually succeeded. I myself loved to be around him, and although I never considered him a deep thinker, I valued his judgment, because he was bright and intuitive. And I firmly believed that he was the best securities salesman I'd ever met.

Beneath the surface, though, he was a troubled person. Full of doubts about himself. Easily frightened, but unwilling to admit it.

9

I didn't know all there was to know about his early life, but I knew a little. His father had been a professional Army officer. Tom had grown up around Army posts in various parts of the United States, Japan and Germany. He'd been destined for a military career and had, following his graduation from West Point, started out on one. But after a few years he'd decided that the Army wasn't for him. He'd resigned his commission, drifted to New York and come to rest in Wall Street.

The decision to leave the Army had been difficult for him. His father was a retired general, his older brother a colonel, his sister's husband a captain. All of them had objected to the move. I'd met General Petacque once, and after thirty minutes with him I'd come away feeling that no one raised under his roof could be entirely normal. For he was, even in retirement, an absolute martinet—a stern, demanding, intolerant, self-righteous ramrod of a human being. According to Tom, his father had always valued two virtues above all others: honesty and courage. Which may have been true. But I couldn't imagine anyone daring to be frank with a son of a bitch like that or strong enough to stand up to him. As far as I was concerned, the general was hell on wheels, and I admired Tom for having survived his childhood as well as he had.

The fact remained, though, that Tom was the sort of guy who, because he's terrified of diving, forces himself to go off the high board but gets the shakes afterward. And when I felt that there might be trouble brewing in some area of the business, I usually discussed it with Mark rather than with Tom, because I knew that Tom would overreact and then try to compensate for having done so.

Yet Mark had had a traumatic childhood, and so had I, and neither of *us* had ever cracked up as Tom had.

The waiter came around. I decided against a third martini and ordered a steak sandwich.

Tom's breakdown occurred shortly after the birth of his son. It began with a mild depression and progressed in stages to acute anxiety. He became afraid to drive a car—he was convinced he was going to have an accident and kill someone. He couldn't sleep. He lost his appetite. He began a wild program of calisthenics that would have tied a professional athlete in knots. And he began to cry when there was nothing to cry about. I realized that something was wrong and tried to talk him into a better frame of mind. Daisy, preoccupied as she was with the new baby, did what she could too. But neither of us could stop the downhill slide. Finally, however, between the two of us we got him to a psychiatrist—Dr. Balter. Dr. Balter felt that the condition was serious enough to require hospitalization.

Once in the hospital, Tom began to improve rapidly. The drugs helped. So did the daily sessions with Dr. Balter. But what really turned the tide was something within Tom himself. Having at last acknowledged the state he'd allowed himself to get into, he fought with all his will to pull himself out of it. If I hadn't admired him before, I certainly would have come to admire him then. I'd seen people claw their way out of the depths. But I'd never seen anyone do it with more determination than Tom.

Within a month he was out of the hospital. Within two months he was back at work. And he went on to become the top salesman in the company, an affectionate husband, a devoted father, a source of strength to friends—including me—when they had problems of their own.

Not that there weren't periods of regression. There were. At times he slid down a few notches. Became gloomy. Exaggerated threats. Lost interest. But those periods never lasted more than a day or two and they never kept him from doing his job better than anyone else could have done it.

Until now.

The steak sandwich came, and I realized why we avoided that restaurant—the meat was like asbestos. I ate as much of it as I could, then paid the check and walked back to the office. The time I'd spent by myself hadn't done me any good. I still didn't know what I was going to say to Tom when I saw him.

I met Brian Barth in the reception room. He was just leaving, he said. He had a long yellow knitted scarf wrapped twice around his neck and dangling over his shoulder, and yellow knitted gloves. He looked like a very large third-grader on his way to school.

I asked him where he was going.

"Over to the Kenwood Building," he replied. "I thought it might be a good idea, sir, to get some more facts about what I was telling you this morning."

"Who are you seeing there?" I asked.

"Wayne Kenwood, sir."

I gaped. Wayne Kenwood was chairman of the board of the multibillion-dollar company. Even I'd never met him. "How in God's name did you get an appointment with Wayne Kenwood?"

"I just called him up."

I didn't know whether to be angry or amused. I was a little of both. "Don't you think that was rather presumptuous of you?"

"Yes, sir, it may have been." He gave me a cherubic smile. "But it worked."

I wanted to warn him to be careful about what he said to Kenwood. I didn't, though. For it occurred to me that with Brian Barth across the desk from him, perhaps it was Kenwood who should be careful. "Well, good luck," I said, and, somewhat bemused, I continued down the corridor to my office.

I made a few notes for the Tuesday letter. The letter wouldn't actually be written until the next day, to allow for last-minute developments if there were any, but I wanted to decide what should go in and what should be left out. Then I remembered that I hadn't made plane reservations for the trip to Dallas. Although I'm head of the research department at Price, Potter and Petacque, I'm also one of the researchers. My specialty is insurance companies, and I had a date on Wednesday to see some of the executives of Great Southwest Life and Casualty Company.

I told Helen to get me on a flight that left on Tuesday evening. She reported back in a few minutes that the reservation was made. Then gave me the flight information, and added that there was a call for me on line two.

"Who is it?" I asked.

"Mrs. Petacque."

I quickly pushed the button for line two. "Daisy?"

"Is that you, Brock?"

"Yes. I'm glad you called. I—"

"Do you know where Tom is, Brock? I've been trying to reach him since eleven o'clock. His secretary keeps telling me that he's out and she doesn't know when he'll be back."

"That's right. He left a little before eleven. What's wrong with him, Daisy?"

There was a slight pause. "Wrong?"

"He seemed pretty upset this morning."

There was a longer pause. "I don't know." Then there was a catch in her voice. "Oh, Brock, I'm terribly worried about him!"

"So am I. He wasn't himself at all."

"I know. I don't know what to do."

"I was thinking that maybe I could come over this evening and have a little talk with him."

"Oh, I wish you would! Maybe you can find out what the trouble is." She sounded close to tears.

"It might help if I had a little talk with you first, though. Where are you right now?"

"I'm home. I've been afraid to leave. Afraid he might call or something. When he left this morning—" She began to sob.

"Now, now, Daisy, don't do that. Please. If you and I could get together for a few minutes, we might be able to figure it out."

"I'm afraid to leave, in case he comes home or calls. I don't know where he is or what he's planning to do."

"What do you mean, you don't know what he's planning to do?"

"He—he's never been like this, Brock. It's worse than it's ever been."

"I'll come over to your apartment."

"If he came home and found you here, he might think . . ."

"O.K. Meet me at the Plaza, then. The Oak Room." I glanced at my watch. "Say around four o'clock."

"Suppose he comes home and I'm not here."

"You'll be back by five."

"You don't understand, Brock. He"—her voice rose almost to a wail—"he's got a *gun.*"

"What!"

"He's got a *gun,* Brock. He took it with him this morning."

"Forget about the Oak Room. Stay where you are. I'll be at your place in fifteen minutes."

I slammed down the telephone, grabbed my coat and ran.

–3–

Traffic was fierce. The trip uptown, instead of taking a quarter of an hour, took thirty-five minutes.

Jerry, my godson, opened the door. He had a half-eaten apple in his hand and appeared cheerful enough. He could now do, he told me, three complete somersaults on the parallel bars, whereas before Christmas he hadn't been able to do even one.

I congratulated him and asked whether his father was home. He shook his head.

"Where's your mother?"

"In the bedroom. I'll get her."

"Never mind. I'll get her myself."

"Be careful. She's in a ba-a-a-d mood."

"Thanks for the tip."

He ambled off in the direction of the kitchen, and I went to the bedroom. The door was closed. I knocked. A moment later the door opened. Daisy threw herself into my arms, uttered a couple of stifled sobs, then backed away.

She looked terrible. For her, that is. She was a gorgeous woman.

14

She'd once been a fashion model. One of the best. Cover of *Vogue*, cover of *Harper's Bazaar*, the works. She could never look truly unattractive.

"Any word yet?" I asked.

"No." Two more stifled sobs. Then she pulled herself together. "I'm simply beside myself."

"Tell me about the gun."

She took me by the hand and led me over to the window side of the room, where two chairs flanked a small glass coffee table. On the table was the Limoges coffee set I'd given to Daisy and Tom for their fifth wedding anniversary. One of the cups had coffee in it.

"Tell me about the gun," I repeated as we sat down.

"I don't know where he got it. I didn't even know he had it. It's a horrible, ugly little thing." Without asking, she poured coffee into the other cup, then said distractedly, "It's a bit cold, I'm afraid."

"When did you first see the gun?"

"Saturday night. Or rather yesterday morning. About three o'clock. I woke up. Tom wasn't in bed. I went looking for him. I found him in the den. The gun was on the desk. He was sitting there, staring at it. I couldn't believe my eyes. 'Where on earth did you get that?' I said. He looked at me in that funny way he has. 'Go back to bed,' he said. 'Leave me alone.' I thought—well, God knows what. 'I won't go back to bed,' I said, 'and give me that hideous gun.' He wouldn't, and we started to quarrel. Not really quarrel, exactly—he was in one of those unresponsive moods when you can't quarrel with him, no matter how hard you try. But I was angry and frightened and I told him I wasn't going to have any gun in the house, not for any reason whatsoever. Anyway, after a while I made him give me the gun and I hid it. I put it in the closet, in the box with the mink stole I don't wear anymore. I didn't think he'd find it there. But this morning I went to get it—I was going to throw it out—and it was gone."

"Maybe somebody else took it."

15

"Who? There was nobody in the house yesterday except Jerry, Tom and me. Laura Laverne was off."

"Laura Laverne?"

"The new maid. She refuses to work weekends."

"And Jerry?"

"He wouldn't go prowling in our closet. I didn't want to come right out and ask him—I didn't want him to know it was there —but I know he wouldn't."

I thought of burglars. Also of a planned suicide attempt. A planned suicide attempt, under the circumstances, seemed more plausible. But what were the circumstances?

"Has he been slipping into one of his down periods?" I sipped some of the coffee. It really was cold.

"No, he's been fine. Until Saturday night, that is. From then on—well, yes."

"Saturday night?"

"Ray came over. He's in town for a few days. The two of them had a fight."

"His brother Ray?"

Daisy nodded. "He called up Saturday afternoon. He'd just flown in from Phoenix. I invited him for dinner. He came. And after dinner the two of them got into a fight."

"What about?"

"I don't know. They were in the den. Private business, they said. I went into the living room and watched television. I could hear raised voices through the closed door, but I couldn't hear what they were saying. And about ten o'clock Ray stalked out of the house. He didn't even say goodbye to me. I asked Tom what in the world had happened. He wouldn't tell me. But from then on he hasn't been the same. Oh, Brock, what are we going to do!"

"We're going to find out what the trouble is, that's what we're going to do."

"But suppose . . ." She couldn't bring herself to voice the rest of it.

16

"He won't kill himself." I managed to sound more convinced than I felt.

"How do you know?"

"Because I do." I said it without having a reason. Then one came to me. "This morning he gave Mark and me an ultimatum. He said we had forty-eight hours to make up our minds. So I assume that, whatever he has in mind, he isn't planning to do anything for at least two days."

"An ultimatum? What kind of ultimatum?"

I hesitated, then decided to tell her. "He wants us to buy him out."

"Oh, dear God!"

"And it doesn't make sense, Daisy. Everything's been fine between him and Mark and me. There're no problems."

"But don't you see? He really is planning to kill himself and he wants to leave his estate liquid. I think we ought to call the police."

"And then what?"

She gave a deep and uneven sigh.

"One man walking around the streets of New York with a gun in his pocket—if he has the gun in his pocket—isn't going to get them very aroused. And one man, among all the millions—it'd be hopeless."

"I suppose you're right." She sighed again.

"Besides, if what you're thinking is true, we've got at least forty-eight hours, and possibly longer. Mark and I aren't going to buy him out and we aren't going to let him sell to anyone else either if we can possibly prevent it. We can stall him for a hell of a long time."

"Thank goodness for that. But still . . ."

"All we can do is wait, Daisy. He'll come home. I'm almost sure of it."

"I called Dr. Balter," she said presently.

"What did he say?"

"Nothing. Tom had been to see him last week. He seemed all right then."

I nodded. But I made a mental note to talk to Dr. Balter myself.

Laura Laverne came into the room. She wanted to know whether she should go ahead and put the roast in the oven.

Daisy told her she should, then turned to me. "You'll stay for dinner, won't you?"

"Yes."

The maid left. Daisy and I sat in silence. Cold as it was, I finished the coffee and poured myself some more. I drank that too. I avoided looking at Daisy and tried not to think of what might have been.

What might have been is that Daisy might have divorced Tom and married me. Or so I fantasized. It probably wouldn't have happened. But there'd been a moment—a single moment—when, I believed, the possibility existed.

It was the day after Tom went into the hospital. Daisy was distraught. I was at their apartment, doing what I could to console her. We were sitting side by side on the couch. I was holding her hand. Suddenly she leaned against me. I put my arm around her. She let her head rest against my shoulder. Then she half turned and raised her lips. I kissed her. It wasn't a casual kiss. There was passion in it. Mutual passion. We clung to each other. But finally she broke away. "Tom deserves better than this, Brock," she said hoarsely. "I know," I said. And that was the end of it. For the baby awoke and started to cry, and Daisy went in to give him his bottle.

We soon managed to get back to our former relationship, affectionate and friendly. Neither of us ever spoke of what had happened that night. I persuaded myself that I was glad things had turned out as they had. But every now and then I found myself wondering what it would have been like if the pendulum, at that instant, had swung in the other direction.

Now, as if she knew what was running through my mind, Daisy said, "I love Tom very much, Brock."

18

I put down the coffee cup that I was still holding. "So do I, dear. He's the closest thing to a brother I've ever had." I paused. "Which reminds me: what hotel is Ray staying at?"

"I don't know. He usually stays at the Park Lane."

"I'll call. I'm sure he can throw some light on whatever it is that happened."

"I thought of that. I was afraid, though. I didn't want Tom to think I was interfering."

"Well, let's not worry about that." I went to the telephone and called the Park Lane.

Colonel Ray Petacque wasn't registered. Colonel Ray Petacque hadn't been registered on Saturday or Sunday. Sorry, sir. Thank you for calling. Good afternoon.

I gave Daisy the information.

She groaned. "There are so many other hotels, I wouldn't know where to start."

I didn't know either. "I could use a drink," I said. "The coffee's like ice."

We went into the living room. Jerry was sprawled on the floor. Instead of an apple, he was now munching on a slice of salami. There was a radio beside him, and he had the headset plugged into his ears. A book lay open in front of him. I bent down to see what it was. It was a book about ocean liners. He was studying a full-page photograph of the *Aquitania.* Noting my interest, he removed the headset and said, "I like the *Queen Mary* better.

"Why?" I asked.

He turned some pages and showed me a picture of the *Queen Mary.* Biting off a piece of salami, he said, "Nicer chimneys."

"Smokestacks," his mother corrected him. "And don't talk with your mouth full."

He plugged in the headset again. I made drinks for Daisy and myself.

"The roast won't be ready for hours," she said.

"Then we'll get drunk," I said.

She gave me a wan smile.

19

We remained in the living room and, for Jerry's benefit, tried to act as if nothing was wrong. After a while he closed the book, turned off the radio and joined the conversation. We covered a range of subjects, from the stock market, in which he had a precocious but understandable interest, to the latest painting I'd added to my collection, in which he had no interest whatsoever but which Daisy wanted to know about.

It was, to all outward appearances, a fairly normal late afternoon. And the dinner hour, when it finally arrived, seemed fairly normal also. But apparently nobody was fooling anybody, least of all Jerry, for just as we were about to get up from the table he said, apropos of nothing, "Pop's going crazy, isn't he?"

Daisy was too startled to come up with a reply.

I did the best I could. "No," I said. "But he has some heavy problems, pal, so leave him alone."

Jerry nodded, and we left the dining room.

I remained at the apartment until ten-thirty.

Tom still hadn't come home.

At that point I decided that I'd better get Mark into the act. I was genuinely scared. More than most people would have been. For when I was nine years old my father had committed suicide.

– 4 –

Tom's apartment is at Sixty-ninth Street and Third Avenue. Mark's is at Seventy-fifth Street and Fifth Avenue, and it's something special. A ten-room duplex overlooking Central Park which at one time belonged to the United States ambassador to Belgium. A vast place with a two-story living room, a kitchen the size of the skating rink at Rockefeller Center and a curving staircase broad enough to accommodate five people abreast.

It's furnished with an assortment of antiques culled from the various houses Mark's and his wife's parents once owned or still

20

own, which don't quite fill it, and with odds and ends acquired at Sears, Roebuck and Macy's bargain basement.

For when it comes to money, Mark is, to put it kindly, eccentric. And his wife, Joyce, who's wealthy in her own right, is just like him. In addition to the apartment in New York, they have a five-acre spread in Greenwich, Connecticut, and a sixty-foot yacht. But in everyday matters they're the stingiest couple I've ever known. As their guests you drink wine from goblets of Waterford crystal, but it's the cheapest wine on the market. Rather than pay five dollars to park in a garage, Mark will drive around for twenty minutes, looking for a free parking space on the street. At the theater he and Joyce sit in the balcony. For them a spending spree means buying six handkerchiefs.

It wouldn't be so bad if Mark were only stingy at home, but he's like that at the office too. He examines every bill that comes in and questions even the most trivial expenditures. Which causes trouble with employees, suppliers and customers. He suspects everyone of trying to cheat us.

Yet he's a hell of a worker, he's scrupulously honest himself, he's a devoted husband and father, he's a loyal friend, and on occasion he can be quite generous.

And while I keep hoping that someday he'll really loosen up, I doubt that he will. Except that maybe when his father dies and leaves him another fifteen or twenty million, he'll go out and buy himself a new raincoat—God knows, he needs one.

At any rate, he greeted me that evening in his usual at-home outfit, bluejeans, a frayed sweater and rubber thong sandals.

He took one look at me and said, "Trouble?"

I nodded and said, "Tom."

He led me into the library and closed the door. I told him what had been going on. I added that maybe, as Daisy had suggested, we should call the police.

His reaction was the same as mine had been earlier. "What could they do?"

"They could check the hospitals," I said, "and places like that."

21

"What places like that? You mean the morgue?"

"Perhaps."

He regarded me gravely. Then his expression changed. He seemed to be looking not at me but at some recess deep within himself. "Tom isn't dead," he said finally.

"What makes you so sure?"

"He gave us forty-eight hours, remember?"

"That's what I told Daisy. But even so."

He again withdrew into himself. And again emerged with a positive statement. "Tom is not a self-destructive man."

"I've known him longer than you have, Mark."

"Granted. But I repeat, he's not self-destructive. I never would have accepted him as a partner if I'd thought he was. And his performance proves me right. Self-destructive people are failures. Tom is a success."

I thought that over. It didn't seem to me that he was altogether correct.

"I don't know why he's suddenly taken it into his head to start carrying a gun," Mark went on, "and I'll concede that he's going through some sort of emotional crisis, but I don't believe for one minute that he's sitting alone in some hotel room tonight, trying to get up the nerve to blow his brains out."

"Then what is he doing?"

"I don't know, but I think you were on the right track when you tried to locate Ray. If you find him, you may find Tom. And at least you'll find out what the problem is."

"I wouldn't know where to begin looking."

Mark smiled, which was something he seldom did. But when he did smile, he immediately became ten years younger in appearance. And much more likable. "You're the best bloodhound it's ever been my privilege to know, Brock." His smile faded. He reverted to being the Mark Price I knew best—the dour one. "Sometimes you carry things a bit too far and cause unnecessary trouble, but you do manage to come up with information when you set your mind to it."

22

He was referring to a couple of large-scale frauds I'd exposed which had earned me, and our company, the gratitude of a few people and the enmity of many. But I didn't consider myself a bloodhound—and I still don't. "I'm a securities analyst, Mark, not a detective."

"Let's not quibble over words. You're a digger. And I suggest you dig up Ray Petacque."

He had the right idea, I knew. And I didn't doubt that I could handle Ray Petacque when I caught up with him. What bothered me was the simple matter of catching up with him.

There was a knock at the door.

"Who is it?" Mark called.

"It's me," his wife replied, and opened the door. "I thought I heard—" She saw me and said, "Oh, dear!" and clutched at her kimono. The kimono had once been pink, I guessed, but now was a nondescript mauve. She recovered, however, and gave me a friendly smile. "Brock! How nice to see you!" She turned to her husband. "Give Brock a drink, and I'll be right back." She hurried off.

"You want a drink?" Mark asked.

I remembered the quality of the Scotch he'd served the last time I'd been there. "Not particularly."

He made no further effort. We sat in silence, and Joyce returned presently in a hostess gown of green velvet with pearl trim. But some of the pearls were missing, and one of the seams had opened on the right sleeve. She was carrying a plate on which, carefully arranged, were two slices of Swiss cheese and six soda crackers. "No drinks?" she asked.

"Brock didn't want one," Mark told her.

"Well, I'll have one," she said, and Mark got out the bottle.

It ended up that we all had drinks. The Scotch was the same stuff I'd had before, but I managed to get it down. And to eat one of the crackers.

Joyce soon began to sense that something was wrong. "I didn't

23

mean to interrupt you if you were talking business," she said
apologetically.

"We were," Mark said.

"Well, then, I'll go back upstairs." She gave him a fond look
and a kiss. For all their peculiarities, they were a loving pair—and
I envied them that.

Joyce gave me a kiss too. "Don't be such a stranger," she said.
"You haven't been over since Thanksgiving."

"Real soon," I promised.

She left.

I glanced at my watch. It was a quarter past eleven. "I think
I'll call Daisy," I said.

Mark nodded.

Daisy was distraught again. In spite of my advice, she said,
she'd decided to call the police. They were there at the moment.
She was giving them a description of Tom and several photographs of him. They'd promised to circulate them. But they were
of the opinion that Tom was merely on some sort of a bender and
she couldn't convince them that he didn't go on benders.

"Did you tell them about the gun?" I asked.

"Yes."

"What did they say about that?"

"They wanted to know if he has a permit."

"Well, I don't suppose it'll do any harm to have them looking.
But do me a favor, Daisy: give me Ray's home phone number in
Phoenix."

"I'll have to look it up." She put down the telephone. She
returned a moment later and gave me the number.

I wrote it down and told her I'd check with her again, first thing
in the morning. She thanked me and hung up.

I told Mark about the police being with Daisy.

"It won't do us any good if this thing gets into the newspapers," he said. "But I don't suppose it's likely that it will. And
maybe the police will get lucky. Meanwhile, you check with
Phoenix. And I'll see what I can do around town. I don't know

24

all of Tom's haunts, but I know most of them. And someone may have seen him."

On that note we parted. I took a taxi down to my house on West Eleventh Street.

Late as it was, I telephoned Dr. Balter. He'd been asleep, he said. I apologized for waking him and explained the circumstances. He said that he already knew the circumstances, from Daisy. He added that he was aware of nothing that would shed light on the situation. I prevailed upon him, however, to see me first thing in the morning, before his regular office hours. We made a date for seven-thirty.

I then placed a call to Ray Petacque's house. There was no answer.

Finally I went to bed.

I tossed and turned for over an hour but eventually fell asleep. Only to awaken at four o'clock in a cold sweat.

I'd dreamed about a man who'd hanged himself. It was a recurrent nightmare that I'd been having, during periods of stress, since I was nine years old.

But the man in this dream wasn't my father. It was Tom.

– 5 –

Dr. Balter was no stranger to me. I'd been a patient of his myself for a short period of time.

I probably should have gone to a psychiatrist long before I did. And, having started the process, I should have stuck with it. I went to Balter on Tom's recommendation and found that I liked the man. He did me a certain amount of good. But after six weeks I quit. Not because I was unable to face the truths that were coming out, but because I was doing so much traveling that I couldn't keep to the regular schedule of visits Balter insisted upon.

My problem, as I'd guessed beforehand, was the upheaval

caused by my father's death. My father had been raised as a rich man's son, but during the Depression his father had lost every cent. Then his father had died, leaving him to support an invalid mother. Dad had no skills and no talent for making money. Furthermore, he made the mistakes of marrying and of siring a child—me. Eventually the strain of too many responsibilities and the prospect of unending poverty got to him. He put a rope around his neck and kicked the chair out from under him. I came home from school one afternoon to find a crowd of neighbors, police and firemen in our apartment and my mother banging her head on the wall and screaming.

It's easy to make too much of such traumatic experiences, I suppose. To blame them for inadequacies that they really didn't cause. Just as it's possible to bury them too deep, to pretend that they never happened. I'm still not sure to what extent I erred in either direction. But I do know that for years after my father's suicide I grieved, I felt deserted, I was ashamed. And according to Dr. Balter that's why I never married, why I've drifted from one inconsequential love affair to another. I'm afraid of being abandoned.

So my first words to him that Tuesday morning weren't about Tom but about myself. "I had the dream again last night."

"I'm not surprised," was his reply.

"Except that it was Tom who was hanging there."

He nodded.

I then got around to the subject I'd come to discuss.

"I know all that," Balter said presently. "Has anything happened since I talked to you a few hours ago?"

"Not that I know of," I said. "I haven't called Daisy again. I thought she might be asleep, and the poor girl needs whatever rest she can get." I'd told him about the one episode between Daisy and myself. He'd approved of the way we'd handled ourselves.

"Right," he said. "She does." He paused to light a cigar. He smoked them all day long. "But, bearing in mind that no one ever knows what someone's liable to do when they're in the condition

26

Tom's evidently in, I wouldn't be as alarmed as the two of you seem to be."

"What do you mean, 'evidently'? The guy's cracked up and is walking around with a gun!"

"The gun, of course, is serious, and I'm not minimizing what you tell me. But Tom was here last Thursday and he had none of the symptoms of a man who's cracking up, as you put it."

"He had a fight with his brother Saturday night, and something his brother said pushed him over the edge."

"That's possible. But you may be making too much of the whole thing."

"I respect your opinion, doctor, but I don't think I am. I saw him yesterday morning, and you didn't."

"Describe exactly how he looked and what he said."

I did.

He reflected. Finally he said, "There's no doubt that since Saturday night he's been under pressure of some sort. And frankly I'm surprised that he didn't call me. Usually, even apart from his weekly visits, he does when something is troubling him. But without betraying our doctor-patient relationship, I think I can assure you that Tom isn't a suicidal person. He never was."

"That's what my partner Mark said. But what the hell, Dr. Balter, anyone, pushed hard enough, can become suicidal."

"You're projecting."

"If you say so. But I think, at the moment, I'm right."

He spilled ashes on his tie, which was something else he did all day long. "Tom," he said, "has more than his share of hostilities. But he's not the kind to take them out on himself. At least not in that way. Quite the contrary. I'd be inclined to say that, given enough pressure, he'd be less apt to kill himself than he would be to kill someone else."

I gaped. "You mean he'd be capable of committing a murder?"

He gave me a thin smile. "Theoretically, we all are. Most of us don't, however."

"You're crazy!"

27

His smile broadened. "Really?"

I felt myself blushing, and I don't often blush. "I'm sorry. I didn't mean that. But Tom isn't one of those people who loses his temper. He doesn't holler or get overly aggressive or anything like that. Honestly."

"He is aggressive, though, wouldn't you say?"

"Yes."

"All aggressive people, all hostile people, aren't fist-shakers and desk-bangers, you know. But, as I said before, Tom's hostilities are not expressed toward himself. Not, if you don't mind my saying so, as much as yours are."

"Then you think that Tom may be planning to kill someone?" I couldn't believe it.

"Who knows? Planning, perhaps. But it isn't likely that he'll do it. I've been in practice for thirty years, Brock, and none of my patients has ever committed a murder, although plenty of them have wanted to at one time or another."

"I hope to God the police catch him and lock him up, then!"

"Before, rather than after, you mean."

"Naturally."

There was a buzz. I recognized it as the sound which indicated that the next patient had arrived. I didn't want to leave. I wanted to stay there and talk some more. But Balter put his cigar in the ashtray and got to his feet, so I rose too.

"Try to keep your sense of perspective, Brock," he said reassuringly. "I'm concerned, as you are. But I've known Tom a good many years. I believe he'll come through this all right."

I sighed heavily. "I hope so."

He opened the door for me. "Keep in touch. Let me know as soon as there are any further developments."

I nodded. I felt somewhat better. For it was inconceivable to me that Tom would ever, under any circumstances, commit a murder.

−6−

It had started to snow. Big, wet flakes that melted on contact and felt like rain.

I walked down Park Avenue from Eighty-second Street to Sixty-first, then over to Lexington. Damp and chilled, I went into a coffee shop and ordered a cheese Danish and coffee. There was a pay phone in the back of the shop, and when I finished eating I called Daisy.

The maid answered and said that Mrs. Petacque was asleep. But while she was saying it, Daisy picked up the extension and said, "Tom?"

"No," I said. "Brock."

"Brock?" she repeated as if the name were unfamiliar to her.

"Are you up?" the maid asked her.

"I guess so," Daisy replied.

There was a click as the maid put down her telephone.

"Brock?" Daisy said again.

"Yes," I said. "Any word from Tom?"

"I took two Seconals. My head feels like yarn. Tom? No—nothing. I called the police last night."

"You told me that."

"I did?"

"Yes. Have they found out anything?"

"No. I haven't heard from them." Her voice grew stronger. "Oh, Brock, I'm so dreadfully worried!"

"Well, take it easy. I've just been to see Dr. Balter, and he says there's nothing to worry about—Tom isn't the suicidal type. He thinks we're making too much of the whole thing."

"Tom's never stayed out all night before."

"There's probably a damn good reason, but it's not the reason we've been thinking. And Balter's a good man—you know that. How's Jerry?"

"What time is it?"

"A quarter to nine."

"He must have left for school already."

"Well, keep an eye on him. This is liable to be kind of upsetting to him too, you know."

"I know. And I will. You're a lamb, Brock. You really are. I don't know what I'd do without you."

I felt a catch in my throat. It didn't last, though. "I'm on my way to the office now. Call me if you hear anything."

"I will. And thanks, dear. Thanks for everything." She hung up.

I left the coffee shop and hailed a taxi.

I'd barely hung up my coat when Irving came storming into my office. "You've got to do something about Brian," he said angrily. "All hell broke loose yesterday after you left."

I tried to switch on my normal office mentality. "What kind of all hell?"

"I got a call from Jack Watson over at Kenwood Oil. Evidently Brian somehow got himself an appointment with none other than Wayne Kenwood, and I don't know what Brian said to the old man, but the old man is livid. Watson said that he has instructions to bar anyone from our company from their offices. Any news they have to give out, as far as they're concerned, we can get from reading the newspapers."

I sighed. My normal office mentality was working, but not at full strength. "I wouldn't get too excited about it, Irv. Any good news they have to release they'll release to us the same as to everyone else. And the bad news they'll keep to themselves anyway."

"But somebody's got to put that kid in his place. He can't go around thinking he's some kind of law unto himself. If you don't, I will."

"O.K., Irv, I'll speak to him." I sighed again. "No, on second thought, you do it. I'll call Watson and apologize."

Irving calmed down. He gave me another of those owlish looks. "Brock, I know it's none of my business, but I have the feeling that something's wrong. If I can help in any way . . ."

"No. Now beat it. I have work to do."

He started to leave.

I called him back. He was completely trustworthy, and I did need help. "I'm sorry, Irv. I didn't mean to be so abrupt. Something is wrong, and there are things you can do."

I gave him a rundown of the situation. I knew he'd let himself be drawn and quartered before he'd repeat a word of it to anyone without my permission.

He listened quietly, then said, "I'm sorry, Brock. For Tom and for all of us."

I forced a smile. "It isn't as bad as all that, Irv. Mark and I aren't going to let him sell. There are plenty of roadblocks we can put in the way. And eventually Tom'll come to his senses. He's a pretty sturdy guy, you know. But there are a few things you can do for me. First of all, here are the notes I made for the letter that has to go out this afternoon. You write it. Then I'm supposed to go to Dallas tonight to see Henderson at Great Southwest. You make the trip for me. I'll call and explain that I have the flu or something. I'll brief you on the information I'm looking for."

Irving's eyes widened. It wasn't unusual for me to let him write the weekly letter when I was otherwise occupied, but I'd never let him, or anyone else, deal with the insurance companies, which I felt were my special province. "Of course, boss," he said enthusiastically. He only called me "boss" when he was deeply stirred. "Anything else I can do?"

I thought for a moment. "Maybe. There's something that's been bothering me ever since last night. Have you heard any rumors about Mutual Claims?" Mutual Claims Company was the outfit of which Ray Petacque, since his retirement from the Army, had been vice-president.

Irving shook his head. "No, I haven't. You think there could be some connection between Mutual Claims and the way Tom's acting?"

"I don't know. I can't think of any. It wouldn't hurt to check around, though. Quietly, of course."

"Of course." No one could be more quiet than Irving, when he chose to be. "Will do. And"—he hesitated—"thanks, boss. I appreciate your confidence."

I waved him away. He went happily. I headed down the corridor to see whether Mark was in his office. He wasn't. Rose Frank, his secretary, said that he'd called in to tell her he'd be late.

"I hope he's not sick," she added.

I could understand her concern. Mark was invariably the first one to show up in the morning. "I'm sure he's not," I said. "He mentioned something yesterday about having an appointment."

She looked relieved.

I pictured Mark going from place to place, pursuing his inquiries. I smiled. He really wasn't the type for that sort of thing. He was too stand-offish. "Let me know when he comes in, though," I said.

Rose wrote herself a note to do so. She wrote herself notes about everything. Mark insisted on it.

I returned to my office and placed a call to Ray Petacque's house. It was seven in the morning in Arizona. Someone would have to answer.

But no one did.

I decided to wait until nine o'clock, Arizona time, and call Mutual Claims. If Ray wasn't there, I could talk to Steve Schroeder. Steve Schroeder was founder, president and chief executive officer of the company. He might know where Ray was.

After that things got really hectic. With Tom and Mark away, everybody began to bring his problems to me. I found myself making decisions on matters I knew little about. Furthermore, Hardin Webster called. Hardin was with Amalgamated Investors Services, in Boston. Amalgamated was one of our largest customers. We handled almost a hundred million dollars' worth of their trading per year. And Hardin was an eager beaver. He often called on Tuesday morning, to try and worm out of me advance information about what was in the letter that was to go out on Tuesday afternoon. It was a touchy situation. I couldn't afford to antagonize him and I couldn't in good conscience give him information ahead of the other customers. I handled the matter in my usual way, by giving him other information. Then someone from *The Wall Street Journal* called. He'd heard that we were working on an in-depth study of grocery chains and wanted to know when it would be ready for release. I had to ask George Cole, the one who was working on the study, and get back to the man at the *Journal.*

Periodically I checked the ticker tape, but there was no exciting information on it. The exchange was having another dull day. With it all, however, I managed to squeeze in the call to Henderson, in Dallas, and explain that while I had a bug and couldn't come to Dallas myself, my number-one boy, Irving Silvers, would be there in my place. And the apology to Jack Watson at Kenwood Oil. It took fifteen minutes to convince him that I was truly, deeply, abjectly, even desperately sorry for the behavior of the new member of my staff, who was still in training and who had been severely reprimanded. Watson seemed satisfied and said he'd convey my sentiments to the chairman of the board.

I hung up, swore aloud several times and went back to work.

No word from Daisy.

No word from Mark.

I placed a call to Mutual Claims Company in Phoenix.

I was told that Mr. Petacque was out of town. And that Mr. Schroeder was out of town also.

I began to think about a private investigator I knew. His name was Philip Quick, and he lived in Chicago. I'd used him once, when I was trying to uncover one of the insurance frauds. He was an annoying man, but he was amazingly good at his job.

I went through the stack of business cards that I kept in the middle drawer of my desk. I found Quick's. I gazed at it and wondered whether things had really reached the point where I needed a private investigator.

I was still trying to make up my mind when the telephone rang. "Who is it?" I asked irritably.

"Mr. Steven Schroeder," Helen replied. "On line one."

I glanced toward the ceiling and said, "Thank you, Lord." Then I pushed the button for line one.

"Brock? Steve Schroeder here. How've you been?"

"Just fine, Steve. And you?"

"Couldn't be better. Look, Brock, I happen to be in town for a few days, and I thought maybe we could get together for lunch today if you're free. I realize it's rather short notice, and if you can't make it for lunch, how about a drink around five? I'm at the Regency."

"You couldn't have picked a better time to call," I said. "I have absolutely nothing on for either lunch of cocktails. Let's make it lunch, though. I'll be delighted to see you."

"Splendid. How soon?"

"Half an hour."

I asked Helen to remain at her desk until I returned and to take all messages. I told her I'd check with her every half hour. She gave me a peculiar look, but said, "Certainly, Mr. Potter."

I offered her my most appreciative smile. Then I hurried out to keep my date with the dumb little man from Phoenix who, in a period of six years, had managed to run a stake of fifteen hundred dollars into a fortune of twenty million.

– 7 –

Steven Schroeder wasn't actually dumb, of course. Nor was he little. He was six feet tall and plenty damn smart. But the image he projected was that of an insignificant and not very bright small-town man who might be capable of handling a simple delivery route but nothing more complicated than that.

In recent years he'd acquired polish. He'd discovered the expensive shops, restaurants and hotels. He'd also learned to talk like other multimillionaires. Yet there remained about him a certain air of awkwardness, of a man in need of guidance. And I tend to be wary of people like that. For I've found that they usually know exactly where they're going.

Nevertheless Price, Potter and Petacque was deeply indebted to Steven Schroeder, and Steven Schroeder was deeply indebted to Price, Potter and Petacque. We'd made a lot of money for each other. Mutual Claims Company was the first issue our firm had ever underwritten, and it was a remarkably successful one for all concerned.

Steven Schroeder was indeed a small-town man, if you call Green Bay, Wisconsin, a small town. At any rate, he wasn't a big-city type in outlook or experience. By rights he should have gone into the cheese business. Green Bay, Wisconsin, calls itself the cheese capital of the world, and Steve's father was a cheese broker. But something went wrong, and Steve began his business career in the accounting office of a hospital.

From Green Bay he moved to Milwaukee, from Milwaukee to Chicago, from Chicago to Phoenix. But he never strayed from his original line of work: hospitals. He had a correspondence-school education in accounting and while he was in Chicago he went to night school to learn computer programming. Then came inspiration.

Steve didn't invent the concept of a company to do outpatient billing for hospitals. Other people were already into it. But he decided to form such a company himself. And he formed one.

It sounded like a nothing-type business when I first heard of it. But I soon learned how wrong I was. A large hospital handles between 250,000 and 500,000 outpatient visits per year. Some hospitals handle as many as a million. Each of these visits has to be recorded, billed and collected for. There's a lot of red tape. Some patients are covered by insurance, others aren't. Some insurance companies pay for one type of treatment but not another. Then there are the complexities of the government agencies that run the welfare programs such as Medicare and Medicaid. The cost of processing a single outpatient visit varies from hospital to hospital, but it may run as high as seven dollars.

An independent company, specializing in that particular field, can do the job for less than half that price and still make a profit.

Furthermore, by using the services of such a company, a hospital not only reduces its billing costs; it becomes more efficient. There are fewer lost checks. Pilferage of money by hospital employees is reduced. Cash flow improves, because less time elapses between the receipt and the deposit of money. And the number of uncollected bills drops sharply.

Finally, a hospital using such a company can borrow against its outpatient accounts receivable, whereas it might not be able to do so otherwise, and hospitals that are trying to raise money for expansion have an easier time raising it. For a company such as Mutual Claims has better financial accountability than the hospital itself.

So when Tom brought Steve to my office the first time and asked me to check into the prospects of Steve's company, and I agreed, I quickly discovered that I was dealing with a new and highly sophisticated type of business that had enormous potential.

But I never imagined that Mutual Claims would grow as fast as it did.

At this point it was servicing some four hundred hospitals around the country, billing seventy-five million dollars annually and netting ten percent of that.

And in the case of Mutual Claims the public was smarter than I was.

Tom had met Steve through his brother Ray. Ray had retired after twenty years in the Army and was looking around to get into business. His path crossed Steve's. Steve was trying to raise cash to start his company. He had fifteen hundred dollars; he needed over forty thousand. Ray invested twenty thousand and talked his father into investing the same amount. Mutual Claims was organized and began to go. But it soon needed money for expansion. Ray, who was vice-president, brought Steve to Tom, and Tom brought him to me. I investigated and was favorably impressed.

Mark, Tom and I talked it over at great length. We were new in the securities business. We'd never done any underwriting. Our capital was limited. I suggested turning the thing over to Price, Underhill, of which Mark's father was one of the senior partners. Investment banking was their specialty. But Mark and his father were on the outs and he refused to go to him; he wanted us to handle the underwriting ourselves. We had several meetings with Steve. Mark urged him to change Mutual Claims into a company that did inpatient billing as well as outpatient billing. Steve explained that it wouldn't work. For while inpatient treatment accounts for eighty percent of a hospital's revenue, the inpatient bills are so large that the cost of processing them is relatively insignificant. It's not the cardiac patient, the cancer patient, the gall bladder patient who causes problems in the accounting departments of hospitals; it's the kid who burns his hand on a stove, the woman who slips on the ice and sprains her wrist, the man who gets a cinder in his eye. The small bills are the ones that overwhelm hospital bookkeepers, not the large bills.

At any rate, we underwrote the issue. I recommended the stock to all our customers, and Tom followed up with a sales pitch. We placed it with every account we had. In addition, Tom, Mark and I bought some ourselves.

The stock came out at $6.50 per share.

Within two weeks it was $14.00.

Within a year it was $46.00.

And then it split.

After the split I recommended that our customers sell. Not because I doubted that the company would continue to do well, but because I'm basically conservative and I don't think that any stock which is selling at thirty-five times earnings is a good value. Our customers did sell. So did I. But Tom and Mark didn't.

I'd never heard the end of it from them, or from our customers. For the stock continued to soar and to split, until the original $6.50 share had reached the equivalent of $156. All our customers had made a lot of money on my recommendation. But they could have made more—and they kept reminding me of that fact.

And I was very much aware of it as I entered Steve's suite at the Regency.

He looked the same as always. Embarrassed.

"Sorry I didn't give you more advance notice," he said, gripping my hand with a firmness that had come only in the last few years. "I didn't know whether you'd have time or not, but I was hoping. Anyway, it's good to see you. How's things?"

"Couldn't be better, Steve. And you?"

"Splendid. Just splendid."

"Splendid" was one of the words he'd acquired at about the same time he'd acquired the firm handshake and the taste for Sulka shirts. I couldn't identify the shirt he was wearing at the moment as having come from Sulka's, but it was silk. And his suit was cashmere. Yet he seemed rumpled. His tie was cockeyed, the suit needed pressing, and the cowlick at the back of his head was standing up like the ear of an angry Chihuahua.

He led me over to the couch. "Drink?" he said. On the coffee table in front of the couch were a bucket of ice, glasses and a bottle of Chivas Regal. Next to the Chivas Regal was an attaché case with all the little interlocked *L*'s and *V*'s that proclaimed it to be the product of Louis Vuitton.

"Don't mind if I do," I said, "but first, may I use your telephone?" It was time, I figured, to check with Helen.

He made an expansive gesture and almost knocked over the bucket of ice.

I dialed my office. "Any messages?" I asked Helen.

"Mr. Price rang. He wanted you to know he's back in the office."

"Let me talk to him."

She connected us.

"Any luck?" I asked.

"None whatsoever. No one's seen him. Where are you?"

"At the Regency, with Steve Schroeder."

There was a slight pause. "Oh?" Another pause. "Does he know anything?"

"I'm not sure. I think maybe."

"See you when you get back."

"Right." I hung up and glanced at the drink Steve had poured for me. He'd practically filled the glass. "You overestimate me," I said.

"A drink should be a drink," he replied.

I noted that he'd poured himself considerably less.

"Cheers," he said, and we clinked glasses.

We fenced. I mentioned that I'd heard that he'd been selling more of his Mutual Claims stock recently. Actually, he'd been selling his stock right along, which was how he'd made part of the twenty million. He'd invested the proceeds in real estate and made big profits in that too. A man has to get his affairs in order, he replied. Which was what they all said. What they meant was that they didn't want too many eggs in one basket. I chided him about not selling his stock through Price, Potter and Petacque. He was sorry about that, he said; his sister's husband had recently moved to Los Angeles and become a stockbroker, and you know how it is with in-laws. I said I knew. He asked me if I was still collecting those funny-looking paintings. I said that I was; I'd bought another Picasso pen and ink sketch and a Jackson Pollock. He said that he wished he could understand things like that, but they just didn't make sense to a country boy like him; he supposed a man could make money as a collector, though, if he knew what he was doing.

I still hadn't finished all the Scotch when we went down to the dining room, and he remarked about that. I told him I was afraid of falling asleep at my desk when I got back to the office.

"You do look kind of tired," he observed. "Been having problems?"

The question seemed innocent, and may have been, but I wasn't sure. "No more than usual," I replied.

The fencing continued over lunch. He was evidently determined to get me drunk, for he insisted we have wine on top of the Scotch. He was just a country boy, he said, and he didn't know anything about wine, but evidently he'd been brushing up on the subject, for the vintage he ordered earned a smile of approval from the headwaiter. While we ate, he regaled me with stories about some of the property he'd bought. The gist of the stories was that, without knowing anything about real estate, he'd innocently stumbled into some pretty good deals. One of them was what he called a little ranchero down Mexico way.

"You like Mexico?" I asked.

"Wasn't there long enough to find out," he answered. "Went down to look the place over, got the shits and came home the next day. Worst case of shits I ever had. It must have been the water. But it turned out to be kind of a nice investment. I've already been offered a profit of half a million."

He kept trying to refill my wineglass. I had a growing feeling that he wanted information of some sort.

I was right, too. But he didn't get around to the subject until the very end of the meal.

"It's been a real pleasure seeing you again, Brock," he said, "and I can't tell you how much I've enjoyed it, but I have to be honest—you were second choice. The one I was really hoping to see was Tom. They told me he was out and they didn't know when he'd be back."

"That's right," I said. "He's away for a few days."

"On business?"

"You know Tom. Everything with him is business."

"Sure, sure. Even horseback riding."

I smiled. Tom was an excellent horseman. His father himself had taught him to ride. "Well," I said, "I'm not proud. I don't mind being second choice."

There was a silence. Steve looked even more embarrassed than before. Finally he said, "I wanted to talk to him confidentially, about his brother. You haven't seen Ray during the past day or so, have you? I believe he was in town."

"Afraid not," I said. "But if there's a message you'd like me to give Tom, I'll be glad to."

He continued to look uncomfortable. But there was something in his eyes that didn't jibe with the rest of his expression. What he was actually doing, I sensed, was sizing me up. "I've always liked you, Brock. I guess I can take you into my confidence. There's something funny going on out our way."

"Funny?"

The eyes which had been appraising suddenly became hard. "I'm beginning to think Ray's a crook."

I didn't have to pretend that I was shocked—I really was. "I don't believe it!"

"Neither did I. But I've been gathering evidence. So when you talk to Tom, tell him to get in touch with me."

I hadn't intended to drink any more wine, but I picked up my glass and drained it. "It seems inconceivable," I said.

"Inconceivable? That's a fancy word, but all right, it's inconceivable. Except that to me it's conceivable as hell."

"What's he done, for God's sake?"

"I trust you, Brock. I guess I've just proved that. But there's a limit to how confidential I want to get with you, and I've already reached that limit. You understand, I hope."

"Well, yes, but—"

"No buts. You know where Tom is, I imagine. You talk to him every day. Tell him to get in touch with me. Here at the hotel."

I nodded.

His expression changed again. He gave me a shy smile. "I hope

41

I haven't upset you." He tossed his napkin onto the table and got up. "Would you like to go into the bar for an after-lunch drink?"

"No, thanks." It was an hour since I'd checked the office for messages, and I was anxious to call Helen. I didn't want to do it in Steve's presence, however.

We went up to his suite and I got my coat. Then I came down to the lobby, found a telephone booth and dialed.

Mrs. Petacque had called twice, Helen said. She wanted me to call her back as soon as possible. It was very important.

I dropped another dime in the slot.

Daisy was ecstatic. Tom was all right. Someone had seen him. At O'Hare Airport in Chicago. Yesterday afternoon.

– 8 –

I heaved a tremendous sigh of relief, and for a moment my legs felt weak. "Who saw him, Daisy?"

"Barbara Mitchell. And it's all a big mix-up. He told her to tell me he was all right, but instead of calling me as soon as she got home she didn't call me until a little while ago—she didn't know I had no idea where he was."

"I see." Barbara Mitchell was a divorcee friend of Daisy's. I'd met her at parties that Tom and Daisy had given.

Daisy went on to explain that Barbara had been in Hawaii. The flight home had stopped in Chicago. Barbara had got off during the layover to stretch her legs. That's when she saw Tom. "I was so happy that I began to cry. I know I made a fool of myself, but I don't care." She sounded as if she was about to start crying again. But she didn't. "What I don't understand, though, is why Tom didn't phone me last night. He always phones me when he's out of town."

"Did Barbara say what he was doing?"

42

"He was sitting in one of the departure lounges, reading a newspaper."

"Was he alone?"

"Alone?"

"Was Ray with him?"

"Barbara doesn't know Ray. Tom didn't introduce her to anyone. I'm sure she'd have mentioned it if he had. Brock, is there something you're not telling me?"

"I believe I know where Tom was going, and I guess Dr. Balter was right—we've been making too much of this whole thing."

"Where?"

"To Phoenix. Evidently he couldn't get on a through flight, so he went to Chicago and was changing planes there. Ray is in some kind of trouble, Daisy, and Tom is trying to help him out. But he doesn't want you or any of us to know about it. That's why he didn't tell us where he was going."

"Brockton Potter, I could kill you! Why didn't you tell me any of this yesterday?"

"Because I just found out about it. And some of it is guesswork on my part."

"He could have told *me.*"

"Apparently he doesn't intend to tell anyone. And, Daisy, don't you tell anyone either. Please."

"Of course not. Is Ray in serious trouble?"

"I don't know. Possibly. But at any rate, Tom will probably be back soon, and I'll have a talk with him."

"I'd better call the police and tell them to stop looking."

"That'd be a good idea."

"Should I call Ray?"

"No. I tried a couple of times. There's no answer."

"Then Blanche must be with them." Blanche was Ray's wife.

"She probably is."

"He didn't mention her on Saturday. I thought he was in New

York alone. He's such a strange man. I never did understand him. He's not at all like Tom."

"Well, leave everything alone. When Tom comes back, Mark and I'll straighten it out."

"If you say so, dear. Oh, I feel so much better!" Her voice broke, and she hung up quickly.

I took a taxi back to the office.

Mark was at his desk. He looked as if he hadn't slept all night.

"I know where Tom is," I said.

He gave me a startled glance.

I described the lunch with Schroeder, then the conversations with Balter and Daisy.

He sat there for a full minute after I finished, saying nothing. At last he said, "Then the reason he's so anxious to sell his interest in the business is that he's afraid there's going to be a scandal and he doesn't want to involve us."

I nodded.

"I didn't think he was that self-sacrificing."

I smiled. "Sure you did."

He permitted himself to return my smile. "I guess I did, at that." He reached into the bottom drawer of his desk and took out a bottle. It was the same brand of Scotch he served at home. "Drink? I feel I could do with one at this point."

I felt that I could too. But not the swill he was offering. "Help yourself," I said. "Me, I'm going back to work."

And I did go back to work. Or at least I tried to. Thoughts of the lunch with Schroeder kept nagging at me. I kept getting interrupted too.

The first interruption was a visit by Brian Barth. He wanted to apologize, he said, for the trouble he'd caused. He looked so crestfallen that I guessed Irving had laced into him and I couldn't bring myself to rub salt in his wounds, so I ended up consoling him.

The next three were questions from men in the sales department, who would normally have consulted with Tom.

The last one was a conference with Irving, who wanted me to see the letter before it went out. I read it, approved it and briefed him on Great Southwest. I was tempted to reverse myself and go to Dallas after all. But I decided that until Tom returned, it would be wise to stick around New York.

At that point, although it was only a quarter past four, I felt I'd had enough aggravation for one day and went home. Where, after a tall drink and a hot shower, I began to unwind.

But unwinding, at times, isn't all that it's cracked up to be.

I began to get lonely.

So I called Carol Fox, who said she had nothing planned for the evening.

I invited her to come over and spend the night.

She said she would.

And she did.

— 9 —

I'd known Carol for a year and a half. We hadn't been able to fall in love and we hadn't been able to break up. If I'd been asked to characterize our relationship in terms of a stock recommendation, I'd have said, "O.K. for short-term appreciation, but no prospect of long-term growth."

And when it came to women, that was the story of my life. A lot of activity but no real development. A rocky road to nowhere.

But I had some nice times along the way, and that night was one of them. Carol's mood and mine meshed, for a change. She worked for a resident buying company—women's apparel—and she too had had a tough day. She was anxious to forget about it.

45

And she was no more eager than I was to think about the problems of the next day.

We spent an hour and a half sipping Scotch in front of the fireplace in my den, deciding where to have dinner. Then we spent two hours having dinner—at the very first place we'd named, a dim little Italian restaurant at the end of the block, which no one ever seemed to patronize except ourselves. Walking home from the restaurant, we met one of my next-door neighbors —Evelyn Natwick. Evelyn was an immigration lawyer. She'd been working late. We talked on the sidewalk for fifteen minutes before coming to the conclusion that that was silly—why didn't we go up to her apartment, where it was warm? So we went up to her apartment, and she broke out a bottle of Remy Martin that a grateful client had given her for Christmas. She regaled us with an account of her day, which had been devoted to frustrating the efforts of the U.S. Immigration and Naturalization Service to deport two construction workers to their native Honduras.

At eleven-thirty Carol and I went back to my house, listened to some Rachmaninoff and hit the sack.

There too we were more compatible than usual.

I slept soundly for several hours, but shortly after four o'clock Carol kicked me, and I awoke.

"What is it?" I asked, startled.

But Carol had delivered the kick in her sleep. She didn't stir.

The light was on. So was the record player. The record was still spinning. Carol's pantyhose were on the floor beside the chair, along with my necktie. I was cold.

I got up, adjusted the thermostat, turned off the record player and the light and went back to bed. I put my arm around Carol and drew her close, but in her sleep she murmured irritably and swung over to the far side of the bed, taking most of the blanket with her. I fought for my share of it. She resisted but eventually gave in, without waking. I tried to get comfortable and more or less succeeded. But I couldn't go back to sleep.

Marriage, I thought.

Years and years of nights with the same woman.

Why was it all right for some but not for others?

There was nothing wrong with Carol. There was nothing wrong with me. We got along as well as most couples. What was lacking?

She turned over abruptly and edged back to the middle of the bed. Her chin came to rest against my arm.

Well, for one thing, she had a sharp chin.

I shifted my position. She put an arm around me and sighed. I felt less rejected.

Nevertheless.

Years and years of nights with the same woman. Mark and Joyce, for instance: seventeen years. Tom and Daisy: eleven years. In spite of all the ups and downs, all the problems.

My thoughts began to stray. Had Tom come home or was he still in Phoenix? Was my guess right—had he really gone to Phoenix? If he showed up at the office, what would his state of mind be?

What the hell had Schroeder been after? If it was information, he'd certainly been disappointed. But was information what he'd really wanted? Why had he told me just so much and no more? Why had he told me anything at all? It almost seemed, in retrospect, that aside from wanting me to put him in touch with Tom, he *hadn't* been after anything. No, that wasn't quite true either. He'd had a purpose. Men like that always had a purpose.

An idea came to me. I discarded it. It returned.

Schroeder had been issuing a warning.

Mark had summed it up, and I'd agreed. There was going to be a scandal, and Tom didn't want our company to be involved. Schroeder had been trying to find out whether I knew that trouble was brewing. But above all he'd been telling me that if something was amiss at Mutual Claims, our company couldn't avoid being affected.

47

And Schroeder was right. We'd been the underwriters; Tom and Mark were still substantial stockholders; Tom's brother was vice-president. Forget about the original underwriting—the Petacque name alone tied the two companies together.

But Ray Petacque a crook? That seemed unlikely. I was in no position to vouch for his character—I'd never got to know him that well. But my opinion, based on the contact that I did have with him, was that he was too uninterested to be a crook. Good crooks spent a lot of time at their work; Ray Petacque spent most of his time playing tennis. And bridge. And supervising the cleaning of his swimming pool.

He made no bones about it. He'd wanted to get into business, but not very actively. The Mutual Claims situation was made to order. Schroeder needed money; Ray needed a source of income to flesh out his pension and an office to go to occasionally. The fact that he'd accidentally become a very rich man didn't alter the basic relationship between him and Schroeder: although Ray held the title of vice-president, he didn't participate actively in day-to-day operations. Schroeder was the brains, the brawn, the energy. Schroeder ran the show.

Besides, why would Ray steal? He had more money than he knew what to do with.

When Tom showed up at the office, Mark and I would have to confront him with what Schroeder had said. We'd work on him together, force him to tell us the truth. We might not be able to avoid the trouble, if there was going to be any, but at least we could prepare ourselves for it.

Suddenly I wanted to call Daisy and ask whether Tom had returned. I switched on the bedside lamp. Carol made a protesting sound and buried her face in the pillow. Ten minutes to five. I switched off the lamp. A telephone call at this hour would frighten Daisy—and Tom too, if he was home. But around eight o'clock it wouldn't. I'd wait until then.

Suppose Tom hadn't returned—then what?

Then another talk with Schroeder.

I began to relax.

I awoke for the second time.

The hands of the clock pointed to seven-thirty. I sat up abruptly. Carol was gone. So were her clothes. I jumped out of bed, opened the bedroom door, listened. Someone was moving about downstairs.

"Carol?" I called.

She came out of the kitchen. "The coffee's on. How do you want your eggs?"

"Over easy." I put on a robe and went down to join her.

There was a variety of utensils on the countertop. The coffee was perking. I poured myself a cup of it.

Carol pushed down the lever of the toaster and came over to me. She gave me a kiss. "Ouch," she said. "You need a shave."

I nodded.

She eyed me. "You were very restless last night."

"How would you know? You slept like a log."

"I did not. I kept waking up."

We began to argue about who was awake and who wasn't. She dropped the eggs into the frying pan. The toast popped up. I took it out of the toaster and put some more bread in.

The telephone rang.

I picked up the kitchen extension.

"Mr. Potter?"

The voice sounded familiar, but I couldn't identify it. "Yes."

"This is General Armand Petacque."

Involuntarily I stiffened. Came to attention. "Yes, sir."

"Mr. Potter, do you know where my son Thomas is?"

I'd only met the man once, but I hadn't thought that I'd ever forget his harsh voice. It was no wonder that I'd failed to recognize it now, though. There was a quaver in it that hadn't been there before. "No, sir. Have you tried his house?"

"I have. I've been dialing that number for an hour. There's no answer."

Daisy's sleeping pills. She'd taken some and pulled the telephone out of the jack.

"It's extremely urgent that I get in touch with my son, Mr. Potter."

"Yes, General. I'll go over to his house. I'm sure someone is home."

"Thank you. Please tell my son—tell him"—his voice broke, but he cleared his throat and went on—"tell him that his brother Ray and his sister-in-law Blanche have been shot to death. Tell him that the funeral will be in Phoenix. Tell him that I myself am leaving for Phoenix immediately to make the arrangements." The general's voice broke once more, and he hung up.

– 10 –

The security at Tom's building was great. The doorman refused to let me in.

"Nobody answers," he kept saying. "Nobody's home."

"Somebody *is* home," I kept insisting. "They're asleep."

I began to kick up a fuss. "This is an emergency," I shouted. "Call the manager."

"There is no manager. The apartments are privately owned. There's a committee."

"Then call the goddamn committee."

"Please, sir. There's no need to raise your voice."

"There is too a need to raise my voice. I'm Mr. Petacque's partner. I have to speak to him or to his wife. I'm not taking no for an answer. The building has a superintendent, doesn't it? Call him."

He finally agreed to call the superintendent. The superintendent gave me the same story. He was not permitted to admit

50

anyone to any of the apartments without the written consent of the owner. I threatened to call the police. That confused both of them. If I was willing to call the police, there was a chance that I might not be a lawbreaker. I repeated the threat. The superintendent thought it over. After a while he agreed to let me into the apartment, provided he came along.

I waited while he went to get the passkey. We went up to the ninth floor, rang the bell, knocked on the door and after an interval entered with the passkey.

No one *was* home.

The bed in Daisy's and Tom's room was unmade. So was the bed in Jerry's room. But there was no sign of anyone.

I stood in the living room and tried to figure out what might have happened. I caught a glimpse of myself in the mirror. I could understand why the doorman and the superintendent had been suspicious of me. I hadn't shaved. I wasn't wearing a tie. My hair needed combing. There was a wild look in my eyes.

"Are you satisfied?" the superintendent asked presently.

"I guess so," I replied.

We rode down to the lobby and I left the building. I went into a coffee shop on Third Avenue and called Mark at his apartment. Joyce told me that he'd just started for the office. I hailed a cab and reached the office before Mark did.

The switchboard operator was taking off her coat. She started to say good morning but ended up staring.

Ward Carlton came out of the men's washroom. He was a member of the sales force. He had a copy of *The New York Times* under his arm. He too started to say good morning but ended up staring.

Brian Barth emerged from his office with a mug of coffee and almost bumped into me. He gaped. "Are you all right, Mr. Potter?" he asked.

"Yes," I said, and kept going.

I hung up my coat and went down the corridor to Mark's office.

51

Rose looked up from the note she was writing. She blinked a couple of times but managed to say, "Mr. Price isn't in yet."

"Tell him I want to see him as soon as he comes in," I said. She began another note.

I returned to my office.

Helen appeared. She still had her coat on. "I heard— I— Is there anything I can get you, Mr. Potter?"

"No. Yes. A cup of black coffee, Helen."

She backed out of my office, looking concerned.

A few moments later Mark came in. "Rose said— Good God, man, you look *awful!*"

"I got a telephone call from General Petacque early this morning. Ray and his wife have been shot to death."

Mark suddenly began to look awful himself. "Murdered?"

"Shot is all he said."

Helen returned with the coffee. She glanced from one to the other of us, put the paper cup on my desk and fled.

"Does Tom know?" Mark asked.

"I just came from his apartment. Not only wasn't he there, but now Daisy and Jerry are gone too."

Mark found a chair and dropped into it. He said nothing.

I repeated my conversation with the general and described my visit to Tom's apartment.

Mark sat there, shaking his head. "Where was the old man calling from?" he asked finally.

"He didn't say. His home, I suppose." He lived in Sarasota, Florida. "He's the next of kin. He's probably the first one they notified."

"When did it happen?"

I drank some of the coffee. "I've already told you everything he said."

Mark sighed. "I'd like a cup of coffee too."

I asked Helen to bring him one. She did. But the coffee didn't help him any more than it was helping me.

"I have no answer," he said after a while, and added, "Do you think you ought to go to Phoenix?"

"What good would that do? And why me?"

He shrugged.

We finished the coffee.

"I have a razor in my office, if you want it," Mark said.

"I have one too, somewhere around." I ran my hand over my chin. Jesus.

"Don't you think we ought to talk to Schroeder?"

I considered. "Probably." I called the Regency.

Mr. Schroeder, I was informed, had checked out at eight o'clock.

"He's checked out," I told Mark. "He probably got the word too and is on his way back to Phoenix."

Mark shook his head some more, sighed again and got up. "I'll be in my office if you want me." He left.

I found my razor and went to the men's washroom. Brian was there. He smiled hopefully. "What are you working on today?" I asked.

"Not much, sir. Mr. Silvers was pretty mad yesterday. He said I wasn't to do anything until he came back from Dallas." He colored. "Not even sharpen a pencil."

"Well, I'll give you something to do. Here's ten bucks. Go out and buy me a necktie."

"Yes, sir. I'll be glad to." He took the money and left.

I shaved and combed my hair and returned to my desk. The tempo throughout the office had accelerated; I could feel it. Business went on, no matter what. There was an inexorable rhythm.

I pondered for a few minutes, then fished out the card I'd looked at the day before. I placed a call to Chicago.

The woman at his answering service said that Mr. Quick was out but if I left my name and number he'd call me back. I left them.

Brian came in with the necktie. It was a nice one. "The stores weren't open," he explained, "but I found one that was unlocked."

"You didn't steal, I hope!"

"No, sir. There was a porter who was sweeping up. I promoted him to salesman."

I couldn't help smiling. "Brian, one of these days you're going to be just fine."

"Actually," he said earnestly, "I'm pretty good right now. But Mr. Silvers—"

"I know, I know. You have to learn to control your aggressiveness, that's all."

"But, Mr. Potter . . ." He gazed meaningfully at the necktie.

"You're right," I said. "Aggressiveness is important. So don't change too much. Just a little."

He grinned, gave me my change and departed.

The telephone rang, and Helen reported that a Mr. Philip Quick was on the line, from Chicago.

"Hello, Potter," he said in the self-assured tone of voice that was one of the things I disliked about him. "What can I do for you?"

"I have a job for you."

"Can't handle it today, I'm afraid. I've got four cases on my hands right now. There's a woman—"

"This is important, Quick, so just listen." I was already acquainted with his methods. He worked alone, and never on only one case at a time. "A man named Ray Petacque and his wife were shot to death in Phoenix sometime during the past day or two. I don't know exactly when or where. He was vice-president of a Phoenix company called Mutual Claims. You can probably begin there. I want as many details as you can get about the killings. I'm in no position to go after the information, but you are."

"A couple of telephone calls maybe I could handle."

"That's all it'll take, I imagine. I'll pay you five hundred dollars." He wouldn't touch any case for less than that.

"Well, a couple of phone calls I'll try to squeeze in."

"Good. You can reach me at this number when you find out something. The information is for my ears only, understand?"

"O.K., Potter, O.K.," he said impatiently, and hung up.

I began to breathe easier. At least I'd set something in motion.

The rhythm of office routine began to pulsate around my desk. There were the usual Wednesday morning inquiries from customers about statements made in the Tuesday letter, which they'd just received. Hardin Webster's was one of them. He wanted to verify the statement that the Justice Department was considering antitrust action against Federated Office Equipment. I felt like telling him to ask the Justice Department, but I didn't; I told him that that was what one of my people had heard. When he finished talking to me he asked to be connected to Tom. I said that Tom wasn't in. I persuaded him to settle for Ward Carlton.

It got so hectic that after a while I told Helen to see whether she couldn't transfer some of the calls to other members of the department. She said there was no one to transfer them to—Mr. Rothland was in Philadelphia, Miss Jensen was in San Francisco, Mr. Cole was on his way to Baltimore, and Mr. Silvers was in Dallas; the only one around was Mr. Barth, and Mr. Silvers had left instructions that Mr. Barth wasn't to talk to customers. I was tempted to countermand those instructions, but I let them stand. And I realized, as I always did when Irving was out of town, how much I'd come to depend upon him. I'd made it a rule that the two of us couldn't be away from the office on the same day. I decided now that although the rule was good, it had its drawbacks, especially when I was the one who had to stay in and take the heat.

At ten-thirty I asked for another cup of coffee. Helen brought it. But before it had cooled enough for me to drink, the telephone rang again.

"Who now?" I asked.

"Mrs. Petacque," Helen replied. "Line one."

In my haste I pushed the wrong button and got a buzz. I corrected the mistake immediately. "Daisy? Where in God's name are you?"

"In Great Neck, at my sister's. Jerry is with me. We're in danger, Brock."

— 11 —

The door to Mark's office was closed.

"He's in conference," Rose said.

I started to go in anyway, but the door opened before I reached it. A short, stocky man whom I'd never seen before came out of the office, accompanied by Mark. Mark didn't introduce us.

The man said, "Thank you very much," and the two of them shook hands. Then the man left, and Mark motioned for me to follow him into his office.

I did. "Daisy just called," I said. "She and Jerry are in Great Neck with her sister. Tom told her they were in danger."

Mark was on his way to the desk. He stopped and spun around. "Is Tom with them?"

"No. He called her last night, around midnight. He wouldn't say where he was, but it was a long-distance call—she heard him dropping a lot of coins into the box."

"He's all right, then?"

"Yes and no. He was very overwrought, she said, and he was insistent that she and Jerry leave the apartment, because they weren't safe there. She tried to get him to explain, but he wouldn't. Finally she gave in. She woke Jerry up and drove the two of them to her sister's."

"Does Tom know where they are?"

I nodded.

56

"Did he say anything about Ray?"

I shook my head.

"Then she doesn't . . . ?"

"I told her."

"How did she take it?"

"She was very upset—naturally. I don't think she was any too fond of Ray, but she did like Blanche. She wanted to go to Phoenix for the funeral, but I talked her out of it. It wasn't too hard, because this seemed to prove that Tom was right and there *is* some kind of danger."

Mark made it to the desk and sat down heavily. "I don't know about that. Tom may simply have been trying to get her out of the way. That man who just left . . ."

"Yes?"

"His name is Lombardi. He's with the New York Police Department. He was looking for Tom."

"For what?"

"To question him." He began drumming his fingers on the desktop. "If there was any doubt about the shootings before, there isn't now. Ray and his wife were murdered."

I gripped the back of the chair that faced the desk. "The police want to question Tom?"

"Urgently. Lombardi didn't tell me too much, but he did say that the New York police have been contacted by the police in Arizona. It may be routine, it may not. But he made no bones about the fact that it was important."

"What did you tell him?"

"The truth. That Tom hasn't been in since Monday morning and I don't know where he is."

"Nothing else?"

Mark shook his head. He continued to drum on the desktop. "Brock, I think you ought to go out to Phoenix. I'd go myself, but in all honesty I'm not as good at this sort of thing as you are."

"That's what I came in to tell you. I've decided to."

He stopped drumming and gave me a thin smile. "I'm glad."

"I've already started the ball rolling. I told Philip Quick to get me all the facts he can."

"The detective from Chicago? His fees are outrageous!" He took a deep breath. "Well, all right. Do whatever you feel you have to. We're all involved in this."

"I'm handicapped by the fact that the key people at Mutual Claims know me. They're liable to be on their guard. Besides, there are two separate problems: finding Tom and learning what's wrong within the company. It's too much for one man."

"Use Quick. You already are, you said."

"He won't leave Chicago. He always has several cases that he's working on at the same time, so he can't get away."

"Are you asking me to go with you? I will, if you think I can help."

"No. Someone has to mind the shop. We can't all be gone at the same time. What I'll probably have to do is hire someone else once I get there."

He nodded, and thought for a moment. "Give me the address and phone number of Daisy's sister. I may take a run out to Great Neck and hang around a bit, in case Tom tries to get in touch with Daisy again."

I gave them to him. He wrote them down. I watched him fold the paper neatly and put it into his shirt pocket. I had a sudden feeling of affection for the man.

He glanced up and saw me watching him. He seemed momentarily embarrassed. "Well, good luck," he said, adding, "to all of us."

I left his office and went down the corridor. I detoured to the ticker tape machine. Ward Carlton was standing beside it.

"Federated Office Equipment is down one and a half," he observed. "I guess that's partly our doing."

I had a sudden thought. "Get me a quote on Mutual Claims."

I followed him to his desk and waited while he tapped out the code letters on his Bunker Ramo telequote machine. "A hundred and forty-one," he reported. "Down three."

"Thank you." The stock had dropped more than twelve points during the past week. I hadn't been paying attention. And I should have been.

I continued toward my office and on the way I passed Brian's. I stopped and went in. Brian was working on the *New York Times* crossword puzzle. Damn it, I thought, this is wrong. We're treating him like a child, and he isn't a child. He's an adult, a damn capable one.

I walked over to him. "Stop that!" I snapped.

He dropped the pen and jumped to his feet.

"I've got a job for you," I said. "Go home and pack. You're going to Phoenix with me. We're leaving this afternoon."

– 12 –

On the plane I told Brian as much as I thought he should know. Which was practically everything. The only items I held back were Tom's panicky attempt to get Mark and me to buy him out and the story of his previous breakdown. Those, I felt, were personal matters.

The speed with which Brian grasped the key facts impressed me. He asked only a few questions, but they were the right ones. They showed once again that his mind was remarkably swift and incisive. More than that, however, they showed that he knew far more about Price, Potter and Petacque than I'd imagined. Including our relationship with Mutual Claims. And he was better acquainted with the capital structure of the Phoenix-based company than I was.

Finally I asked him where he got his information.

"From our market reports," he replied.

I learned, to my astonishment, that during his spare time he'd read every single report Price, Potter and Petacque had ever put out.

59

Furthermore, he admitted, he had in the briefcase under his seat Mutual Claims' most recent financial statement.

My jaw dropped. I hadn't told him until the plane was in the air why we were going to Phoenix. "What made you bring that?"

"I just assumed," he said. "Mr. Petacque hasn't been around for the past couple of days, and as far as I know, Mutual Claims is the only Phoenix company you've ever had anything to do with."

I shut up after that. It just didn't seem necessary to tell him any more.

We crossed the Mississippi River, and the cabin crew began to serve dinner. Gazing down at the frozen farmland thirty thousand feet below, I was struck by the thought that always came to me on transcontinental flights: how vast was the flat table of land that extended from the Allegheny Mountains to the Rockies—the Midwest. How many millions of acres of rich, productive soil there were between Ohio and Colorado, between the Canadian and Mexican borders. Even now, brown and desolate and flecked with snow, the land was awesome. It seemed to go on forever.

I finished my martini. The steward collected my glass. I glanced at Brian and caught him staring at me as if trying to read my mind. He blushed.

"I grew up in the Midwest," I said. "I couldn't wait to get away from it. Now that I have, I sometimes feel I lost something."

He nodded. I didn't think he understood. I wasn't sure I understood either. But then he said, "It isn't moving away from a place that does that, Brock; you'd have had the same feeling if you'd stayed."

I was startled. It was the first time he'd called me by my first name. The relationship between us had evidently changed. And after a moment I decided I was pleased. "Perhaps," I said.

"It comes from getting older."

I smiled. He was right. But I said, "How would you know?"

He frowned. "Everyone always thinks I'm so young. I don't think I am."

60

And at that point the steward brought our trays.

We ate for a few minutes in silence. I began to anticipate. Presently I said, "We'll each need our own car. Tomorrow morning I want you to go over to the Mutual Claims Building. It's on Central Avenue. Start nosing around. Don't do it the way you normally would, though. I don't want Schroeder or anyone else to get any ideas. Apply for a job. Get acquainted with someone. You may not learn as much that way, but you'll learn something. With the vice-president of the company murdered, everyone will be talking. Understand?"

Brian nodded. "Will you call on Schroeder?"

"Perhaps. The first thing I'm going to work on, though, is finding Tom."

"It's a big city," he said skeptically.

"I don't think I'll have a hard time."

He raised his eyebrows.

"Tom's been there often. He has friends. One of them will probably know something."

The pilot announced over the intercom that we were approaching the Rocky Mountains and would be flying over the Sangre de Cristo range. I looked out the window. Since we were flying westward, the sunset had lasted a long while. But now darkness was falling. I could barely see the snow-capped peaks that loomed ahead. To me the Rocky Mountains not only marked the end of the plains, they marked the end of a certain kind of thought. West of the Rockies was the land of optimists.

"Have you ever been West before?" I asked Brian.

"Once," he replied. "When I was sixteen I hitchhiked from Richmond to San Francisco."

"No kidding?" He hadn't struck me as the sort who at any age would have hitchhiked anywhere.

"It was right after my mother remarried," he added, and then lapsed into a silence that I didn't think I ought to intrude upon.

There was some air turbulence. The steward collected the trays.

The plane began to descend. And thirty minutes later the lights of Phoenix appeared in the distance.

– 13 –

The motel was located on Indian School Road, in Scottsdale. I'd stayed there once before, when I couldn't get a room anywhere else, but it wasn't a place where Schroeder would expect to find me. It catered to elderly people of limited means, as well as to the overflow from conventions that were headquartered elsewhere and motorists who were merely passing through town. To the extent that it had a social director and a three-hole pitch-and-putt golf course, it was a resort, but it was a far cry from the more expensive ones, like Camelback Inn or Mountain Shadows.

Nothing seemed to have changed since my previous visit. The bulletin board beside the check-in desk announced bingo at eight-thirty in the Navajo Room and welcomed members of the National Heart Association.

Brian and I were assigned adjoining rooms. I invited him into mine, and we went over the story of the murders that was on the front page of the Phoenix *Gazette*. I'd bought a copy at the airport and we'd already read it once, but this time we really studied it.

The details were grim. Ray Petacque had been shot in the throat and chest. His wife had been shot in the head. Their bodies had been found in the back seat of their Cadillac, which had been abandoned in a thicket in the Salt River Indian Reservation. Two campers, Donald Jennings and Alfred Hurd, had come upon the car and the bodies late Tuesday afternoon and had reported them to employees at the Verde Water Treatment plant, which was nearby, who in turn had notified the Maricopa County sheriff's office. Autopsies had been performed on Wednesday morning, and the investigation was being conducted by detectives from the Mesa substation of the sheriff's office. It was believed that the Petacques had been killed on Monday evening between the hours of eight o'clock and midnight. Bloodstains indicated that they'd been killed in their house on Moonlight Way in the exclusive Paradise Valley Country Estates. The bodies had then been placed in the car and driven to the Indian reservation, apparently in an attempt to delay discovery. It wasn't known whether robbery had been a motive or not; the Petacques had evidently been packing to go on a trip at the time they were shot, and the bedroom was in a state of disorder.

Brian and I took out the maps that we'd been given by the car rental agency. The Salt River Indian Reservation was a large area east of Scottsdale. It was bisected by a major road called Bee Line Highway, which went northeast from Mesa to Payson and Winslow and crossed the Tonto National Forest. We couldn't determine where the car had been abandoned, but we reasoned that since there seemed to be few lesser roads on that part of the map, it had been abandoned not too far from the highway itself, perhaps twenty miles east of the Petacque house.

"Monday night," Brian said thoughtfully.

"Between eight and twelve," I added. Tom had certainly been in Phoenix by then. Yet the newspaper article made no mention of him beyond the statement that he was one of the surviving relatives.

There was a lot about Ray's position in the community. He was described as a "prominent business leader." And his wife as a "popular hostess." But there was nothing about Mutual Claims except the fact that Ray had been vice-president of the company and some words from Steve Schroeder about how shocked he was and how much Ray would be missed.

Brian continued to study the map. "It'd be a long walk back."

I glanced at him.

"I mean, the man who drove the car out there—how did he get back to town?"

"And how," I asked, "did he find the spot in the first place? He'd have to be familiar with the area."

Brian nodded. "I suppose a lot of people are familiar with the area. It's right on the outskirts of the city."

"Yes and no." I couldn't recall ever having been to the Salt River Indian Reservation, but I'd been to some of the other parks and national forests around Phoenix. Some of them had virtually no roads; you could only cross them on foot or on horseback. "Most of those places are pretty rugged. There are a few trails, but that's about all. Tom once told me that a mule is better for getting around in them than a horse is, because it's more sure-footed."

"Mr. Petacque is quite a rider, isn't he?" Brian asked.

I realized what I'd said, and tried to cover up. "Back East, not out here." Then I reminded myself that Brian was on our side. "No, that's not true either. He's been on a couple of short pack trips with Ed Avery."

"I don't suppose it matters," Brian said. "It'd take a lot of doing to get a horse and have it waiting out there, and if he didn't get here until Monday evening . . . Who's Ed Avery?"

"A friend of Tom's." The one I intended to start with.

Brian said nothing. I tried to guess what he was thinking. I guessed wrong. His thoughts had gone off in an altogether different direction. For presently he said, "The profits that Mutual Claims has been making—they've been invested mostly in real estate, haven't they?"

"Those that weren't used for expanding the company, opening branch offices and so on—yes. Why?"

Brian shrugged. He didn't pursue the matter.

Neither did I. "There must be a certain amount of information that the sheriff's office is holding back," I said. "There always is. I'm going to call Philip Quick." I picked up the telephone and dialed.

As usual, the call was taken by Quick's answering service. I left my name and number.

I reread the newspaper story and tried to get something from the photographs of Ray and his wife, which were also on the front page. The resemblance between Tom and Ray was slight. As Daisy had said, Ray had been quite different from Tom. I doubted that they'd had much in common even as boys.

The telephone rang. I answered it.

"Potter? Philip Quick. I tried to reach you in New York a few hours ago, but they said you'd gone out of town."

"I'm in Phoenix. You had information?"

"Naturally." His tone reproached me for even wondering. "All it took was a couple of telephone calls to a guy out there who does what I do here that I've sent clients to. Let me get my notebook out." There was a pause, after which he launched into a recitation of facts. They were the same ones the newspaper had printed, with the addition of the sequence of events following the discovery of the bodies and the results of the autopsy report.

The patrol officer who'd responded to the radio message from the Mesa substation was one Charles Randall. The team of detectives who'd been sent in response to *his* call consisted of two men named Harlow and Eames. A team of ID technicians had subsequently been dispatched at *their* request, and it wasn't until the ID men had finished their investigation that the bodies had been removed to the county morgue and the car towed away for further examination.

Both Ray and Blanche had died quickly. Bloodstains indicated that Blanche had been shot in the bedroom of the house, Ray in the hall, and that both bodies had been dragged through the house to the car. The neighbors hadn't heard any unusual sounds. This was explained by the fact that the houses in the neighborhood were quite a distance apart and the fact that despite ordinances to the contrary, people did sometimes take pot shots at varmints, birds or snakes, and no one thought much of it.

65

"What about the gun?" I asked. The newspaper article hadn't said anything about it.

"They haven't found it, but they've recovered the bullets and they're quite sure they came from a thirty-eight-caliber revolver."

Did Daisy know what kind of gun Tom had been carrying? I doubted that she did. "Anything else?" I asked Quick. I was disappointed. In the past he'd been very helpful, but this time he hadn't come up with anything important.

"Like what?"

"Did your man happen to find out anything about Tom Petacque?"

"Who's he?"

"One of my partners. Ray Petacque's brother."

"You didn't mention *him*. I thought maybe that this Ray was the Petacque in Price, Potter and—"

"No." Unfortunately, other people would probably make the same mistake."

"There was something about a brother, but I didn't make a note of it. You said *Ray*."

"Well, call your man back. The sheriff's office seems to be interested in Tom. I'd like to know why."

"I'll see what I can do. Meanwhile where shall I send my bill?"

"To my office in New York. But get some information on this thing with Tom. It's important. And call me back at this number."

"If my man is in. He may not be. It'll take a while."

"I'll wait."

Only after we hung up did it dawn on me that I could have asked him for the name of the Phoenix investigator and spoken to the man myself.

As it was, I had to wait almost an hour for Quick to get back to me. It was worth it, though. For now he told me what I needed to know.

"They found out that Tom Petacque arrived in Phoenix around

seven o'clock Monday night, but no one has seen him since. They think that's kind of strange."

"How do they know when he arrived?" I asked.

"They were checking car rentals at the airport in connection with another case they're working on. He picked up a Dodge Dart at seven-fifteen Monday night. Had to show his driver's license and a credit card to get it. So then they looked at passenger lists for incoming flights. And now there seems to be something about his having disappeared in New York a couple of days ago. Would you know anything about that?"

"He hasn't been well," I said.

"Anyway, it's a good thing you asked, because my man just learned something else they hadn't told him before. There were two sets of tire marks where the bodies were found."

"Two?"

"One belonged to the Cadillac, the other they haven't identified. But the ID men made impressions of both. What they think is, there was another car parked close by and the killer got away in that. They're looking for the car your partner rented at the airport. They have the license number and the description, but they haven't found it yet."

"Just how identifiable are tire marks?" I asked.

"They're like footprints. Crime labs can often do a lot with them."

"I see. Well, thank you, Phil. Thank you very much. I'll be in touch if I need anything further."

"Any time," Quick said cheerfully, and hung up.

I briefed Brian, and he returned to his own room. I studied the map for a few more minutes. Geographically, Phoenix was a large city, I reminded myself. One of the largest in the United States.

I fell asleep hoping that I was right about Ed Avery.

Our paths had crossed only once. At the housewarming party that Ray and Blanche Petacque gave after moving into the place on Moonlight Way. Tom and Daisy came out from New York for the event, and at their urging I detoured to Phoenix en route home from Los Angeles, where I'd been seeing some insurance executives.

There were at least a hundred and fifty people at the party. But of all those whom I met, Ed Avery was far and away the most interesting.

Tom was the one who introduced me to him, and I gathered at once that there was a special relationship between them. Tom explained that he'd known Ed since he was a boy, when Ed had the house next door to the Petacques' in Wiesbaden, Germany. Ed was a career officer in the Army himself and at that time he and Tom's father were part of the same unit. Although Ed was only a few years younger than General Petacque, he and Tom had struck up a lasting friendship. Tom was obviously very fond of him, and after a few minutes I found myself becoming fond of him too.

His paternal great-grandfather had led a wagon train west from St. Louis. His maternal grandfather had helped build the Santa Fe railroad. His paternal grandmother had been a Navajo Indian. One of his great-uncles had driven a stagecoach for Wells Fargo. Another had been a U.S. marshal. In the hour I spent with Ed Avery that night, I picked up more of the flavor of the old Southwest than I'd picked up from any television show I'd ever seen. Yet he himself was a traveled and sophisticated man who was almost as familiar with Paris, Munich and Tokyo as he was with Paradise Valley. He'd attended the University of Colorado and spent over twenty years in the Army. He'd been around the world twice.

In one respect he was like Steve Schroeder. He enjoyed giving the impression that things happened to him accidentally, through no effort on his part. But whereas Schroeder had no sense of humor at all, Ed did; after a while he let you know that he was putting you on, that he was more than merely the innocent victim of circumstances.

And although he was an easy man to get to know, I had the feeling that he wasn't an easy man to get to know well. There were things about him that even Tom wasn't sure about. His marriage, for instance. At one time there'd been a Mrs. Ed Avery, but Tom had never learned what had happened to her—whether the marriage had ended through divorce or death. He did know that Ed had been forced to retire from active military duty by lung cancer. He'd had an operation, which cured him, and after the operation he'd returned to Arizona and settled in Scottsdale, but on a scale beyond what he could afford on his retirement pay. According to Ed, he'd made money in real estate. This was quite possible; he'd landed back in Arizona in the midst of the population explosion. But he never discussed what his holdings were or how he'd acquired them.

However, if Tom would turn to anyone in Arizona for help, it seemed to me, Ed Avery would be the first person he'd choose.

The address given in the telephone directory was on Scottsdale Road, which was a north-south artery only a few blocks from the motel. It took me a full half hour to find the place, though, for it was several miles north of the center of town, tucked away in one of the many condominium complexes that were springing up all over the desert.

This one was called Villa de la Paz. It consisted of maybe seventy houses which were scattered along a small maze of streets and kept private by a high wall that enclosed the entire community. I parked in the area marked "VISITORS PARKING," which faced a large kidney-shaped swimming pool flanked by shuffleboard courts. A sign in the shape of a hand pointed to the right and said "SALES OFFICE." I located the sales office, but it was closed. Which, considering that it wasn't quite eight o'clock in the morning, was understandable. I wandered around, looking for Ed's house, without success. Finally I returned to where the car was. A building beyond the swimming pool appeared to be some sort of clubhouse. I walked over to it. It too was locked. But while I was standing at the door, it opened unexpectedly and an elderly woman came out. She was carrying a large roasting pan and seemed as surprised to see me as I was to see her.

"My roasting pan," she explained with some embarrassment. "I thought I'd better get it before something happened to it. I loaned it to Rose Wilson. She had a party here last night."

"I'm looking for Mr. Avery," I said. "Ed Avery."

She brightened. "He was at the party."

"Can you tell me which house is his?"

The brightness dimmed. "I'm not sure." She gestured with her head. "Over there someplace. We only moved in in November."

I thanked her and went off in the direction she'd indicated. After a while I found the house. It was the very last one on the street that ran parallel to Scottsdale Road. Like all the other houses, it was white and had a red tiled roof. There was a station wagon in the carport, and attached to it was a horse box.

I took a deep breath, rang the bell and waited. Presently the door opened.

His eyes widened, then narrowed as he broke into a wide grin. "Well, I'll be goddamned!"

"Hi, Ed," I said, grinning myself.

We looked at each other. He hadn't changed. He was the same tall, lean, suntanned Ed Avery that I remembered, with the same shock of improbable curly white hair. But when we'd met before he'd been in party clothes, and now he was wearing jeans, a faded blue turtleneck and cowboy boots with pointed toes. The buckle of his belt was a huge affair of silver and turquoise.

"Son of a buck!" he exclaimed. "Well, come on in!" He stood aside, and I walked into the house.

The living room was large and had a cathedral ceiling. It was furnished in a style that seemed to have less to do with Ed than with some interior decorator, one who liked white and pastels and glass-topped tables. I didn't have much of a chance to see it, however, for Ed took my arm and said, "Come out on the patio and have some coffee," escorting me firmly from the living room, through the dining area and kitchen, into the walled yard where he'd evidently been drinking his morning coffee. "Make yourself at home," he said. "I'll get another cup."

He returned with the cup. He didn't wait for me to tell him why I'd come. "I suppose you're here for the funeral," he said. "Terrible thing. Just terrible." He poured coffee into the cup from an electric pot which was attached to a long extension cord that reached across a pass-through into the kitchen.

I sized him up. He looked concerned but uninvolved. "When's the funeral going to be?" I asked.

He picked up the newspaper which was open on the table beside one of the lounge chairs. "I was just reading about it. Tomorrow morning at ten-thirty." He held out the newspaper.

I put my cup on the brick paving, took the newspaper and sat down on the edge of the other lounge chair. What Ed had been reading was the obituary page, not the story of the murder. I turned back to the news section. The story of the murder had been relegated to page four. It was shorter than the story in the *Gazette* had been; but then, the news was no longer fresh. There was no additional information.

I finished the article and glanced up.

Ed was gazing at me. "I was sort of expecting to hear from Tom," he said. His expression was grave, but there was no trace of deceit in it.

71

"Tom's missing," I said.

"Missing?" His expression didn't change, but there was too much innocence in his voice.

"Missing," I repeated. "There's nothing about it in the newspaper, but the sheriff's men are looking for him."

"Missing since when?"

Yes, too much innocence. "Since Monday morning. Ray was in New York over the weekend. He and Tom had a fight about something. Tom went into one of his depressions. Daisy found him with a gun. Monday morning he came into the office and out of the blue announced that he wanted to sell his interest in the business. Then he walked out, and nobody's seen him since, except a friend of his and Daisy's who ran into him in the airport in Chicago. He was on his way out here. The detectives who are working on the case know that he's here, or at least that he was here. He's either in trouble or he's afraid of something, Ed, but he isn't doing himself any good by hiding."

"I shouldn't think so."

"I'd like to find him, and I'd like your help."

"Of course."

"Ed, you're the first person out here that he'd come to."

"I'd have thought so."

I looked at him. I didn't say anything.

He got the point. "You think he *has* come to me and I know where he is?"

I still said nothing.

"Well, he hasn't."

"Ed, we have to help him."

"You're damn right we do. That boy is like a son to me. At times I felt I was the best friend he ever had. When I first met him he was ten years old, with a bastard of a father that he couldn't even talk to, hardly, without saluting first, and nobody else to turn to. He needed someone like me. I never let him down then, and I've never let him down since. Drink your coffee."

He almost had me convinced, but not quite. I wanted to tell

72

him that there might be a difference between what he considered helping and what I considered helping. I didn't know how to put it, though. I took the coffee cup from the pavement and drank some.

"I'll tell you something, though," he went on. "I'm not going to shed any tears for Ray Petacque. I never much cared for him, even as a kid. I think he was lazy and always looking for the easy way. And the money he made out here went to his head. I'm not glad that he got killed the way he did, and I'm sorry as can be about his wife, because I liked her, but I'm not going to miss Ray *that* much." He snapped his fingers.

"Getting back to Tom," I said.

"Getting back to Tom, there's nothing I wouldn't do for him."

"That makes two of us."

He studied me for a moment, then turned away and poured himself more coffee.

I looked around. The patio was a nice one. The brick pavement was framed by a border of wood shavings, into which a variety of shrubs had been sunk. The wall was of white brick. Beyond it, dominating the complex of houses as it dominated everything for miles around, was the beautifully etched mass of Camelback Mountain. The morning sky was a very deep blue. "This is a hell of a big valley," I said.

Ed grunted affirmatively.

I turned back to him. He was studying me again. "If Tom didn't get in touch with you," I said, "perhaps he got in touch with someone else. He knows a lot of people out here, I imagine. He's always making friends wherever he goes. Can you think of anyone in particular?"

"I always considered that I'd be number one. But sure, I guess there are others. Like the Iversons and the Beckets." He rattled off some other names. "Would you like me to talk to them?"

"I'd rather talk to them myself."

"That might not be such a good idea. If the sheriff's men are looking for him, as you say they are, the word could get around,

73

and then *you'd* be hauled in for questioning. Better let me do it. I could do it without making waves."

I prepared to argue. But before I could say anything further, the doorbell rang.

Ed got up. "Son of a buck, this is my morning for unexpected company." He went into the house.

I followed him.

He opened the door.

"It's been a long time," said General Petacque.

Ed stiffened. "Not long enough," he replied.

– 15 –

The general noticed me standing behind Ed and recognized me. "You're Potter," he said, making it sound like an accusation.

"Yes," I said.

"Where's Thomas?" he demanded.

"I don't know," I said.

"Did you tell him about his brother?"

"I haven't been able to locate him."

"What about his wife?"

"She knows."

"Then where is she?"

"As of right now, I'm not sure."

He addressed himself to Ed. "Are you going to have the courtesy to invite me in?"

A little of the stiffness went out of Ed's spine. He stepped aside.

As the general walked into the living room I got a good look at him. He was using a cane. He'd become a really old man. In addition, he was showing the ravages of grief. But the imperiousness was still there, in his eyes and in the way he held his head. "The police are searching for Thomas," he told Ed. "They think he had something to do with the murder."

"And you agree with them, I suppose," Ed retorted.

The general drew himself up. "You don't have to like me, but I'd appreciate your being civil." He paused. "I have no opinion in the matter."

The two of them glared at each other. I sensed that I was witnessing the resumption of an animosity that went back many years. I didn't know where its origin lay, but suspected that Tom had something to do with it, that decades earlier the two Army officers had competed for possession of a boy's soul. And Ed's next words indicated that they had.

"You always thought the worst of him," he said.

"I'd prefer not to get into a discussion of that," the general said. "The facts are that the police know he was in the area on Monday night and are looking for him. They've told me so. Whatever the truth of the matter may be, he's doing himself no good by hiding. He'd best come forward and face them."

"He hasn't been well," I put in.

The general gave me his attention. "Explain yourself, please."

"He's been somewhat depressed."

The corners of his mouth turned down. "Not too depressed, apparently, to make the trip from New York to Phoenix." He gave his attention to Ed again. "He never was particularly brave, but I'd hoped he'd overcome some of that in recent years."

Ed suddenly seemed to lose his tan. He looked furious. But I was the one who spoke. I was furious too. "Bullshit," I said.

Both of them were startled.

"You don't know anything about it," I added. "I doubt that you ever did."

The color returned to Ed's face. "Bravo," he said.

"You're impertinent," the general informed me.

"So go ahead and have me court-martialed."

He clenched his hands, and for a moment I thought he was going to hit me. He didn't, though.

I made an attempt to overcome my anger. To a degree I succeeded. "I don't want to quarrel with you," I said. "I came out here to find Tom and help him. Ed would like to help him too. The three of us are really on the same side."

He accepted that. "Where is he?" he asked Ed.

"I don't know," Ed replied.

There was a silence. "I find that difficult to believe," the general said at last.

Ed shrugged. "Frankly, Armand, I don't give a damn what you believe."

The general glowered at him. Then he glowered at me. Then he said, "Very well," and walked out of the house.

For a moment, as I watched him go, I felt sorry for him. But only for a moment.

Ed slammed the door. "Bastard!" he exploded. "He was a bastard thirty years ago, and he's still a bastard!" He got hold of himself. "Well, you told him. Good for you." He took my arm and led me back to the patio. "That coffee must be cold. Let me give you some more."

"No, thanks," I said. "But if you'd give me the names of Tom's other friends out here . . ."

He shook his head. "I'll speak to them. It'll be better that way. Trust me."

I looked at him. I still couldn't believe that he didn't have some idea as to Tom's whereabouts.

He seemed to realize what was going through my mind. He smiled. "You made points with me just now. I'm sure you want what's best for Tom, the same as I do. Let me think about it."

"There isn't time, Ed."

He changed the subject. "Where's Daisy and the boy?"

I hesitated.

"Trust me," he said again.

"With her sister."

"O.K. Now, where can I get in touch with you if I have some information?"

I gave him the name of the motel.

"You'll hear from me," he promised. He took my arm once

more. He guided me firmly into the house, toward the front door.

We stopped there. I didn't want to leave.

"Go," he said. "I'll see what's what." He opened the door.

"Please," I said.

He patted me on the shoulder, then gave me a push.

Walking back to the car, I thought of Philip Quick. I wondered whether I could talk him into coming to Phoenix. He was an expert at electronic eavesdropping.

– 16 –

I drove back to the motel. Went up to my room. Felt that I should be doing something, but didn't know what. Thought about Brian; hoped he'd got off to a better start than I had. Tried to remember whether I'd met any Iversons or Beckets at the house-warming party; couldn't; came to the conclusion that Ed had simply made up those names. Got angry.

I went out onto the balcony. It offered a view of Camelback Mountain. I stood there, my hands on the iron railing, looking at that vast bulk of brown rock which was so aptly named; it really was shaped like a reclining camel. Damn Ed Avery.

You're Tom, I told myself. You're scared. You want to hide. You have friends in the area, but one friend in particular. What would you do?

You're Ed Avery. Tom comes to you. You want to help. Brock comes to you and says he wants to help too. What would be your response?

You're General Petacque.

Forget it.

An enormous valley. Hundreds of motels, hotels, guest ranches. An assumed name.

I needed someone like Philip Quick.

77

I walked back into the room and headed for the telephone, but as I reached for it it rang.

"Mr. Brockton Potter?" the operator said.

"Yes."

"I have a collect call for you from Mr. Quick in Chicago. Will you accept the charges?"

"Yes."

"Potter?" Quick said in that abrasive voice.

"I was just about to call you."

"Something came up that I don't know how to handle."

From him, that was a remarkable admission. "What?"

"Finch called me this morning. He's the man in Phoenix who got the information for us. He said he'd had a visit from Harlow and Eames, the detectives who're working on the Petacque case. They'd got wind that he'd been making inquiries. They wanted to know who hired him. He told them me."

I groaned. "Did he have to?"

"Not exactly. What he has to do is live and make a living in Phoenix, and that's easier to do if he doesn't get on the wrong side of the sheriff. Anyway, he did, and a little while ago Harlow called me, wanting to know who *my* client is. Is it all right to tell him?"

"Hell, no, Quick!"

"Are you sure?" He sounded as if he wanted to.

"I've never been more sure of anything in my life."

"Well, all right. They need me more than I need them, so I guess I can stand them off. But I think you're making a mistake. They're going to call me back—I said I had to get the client's permission. When I tell them the client said no, they're only going to get more curious."

I pondered. Quick could say that he'd been hired by the firm of Price, Potter and Petacque. Under the circumstances, that might not appear unusual. Still, it would be better if he held his ground, at least for the time being. "No. Definitely not. How about your coming out here, though? I could use some help."

"No way, Potter. With this wrinkle, I'm not getting any closer to Arizona than I am right now. Besides, I couldn't afford it. I have too many other cases on my hands."

"How about your man Finch? Does he know anything about bugging?"

"I wouldn't call him if I were you."

One more avenue with a barricade across it. But Quick was right. "Very well. Whatever you do, though, keep my name to yourself. Understand?"

"O.K., if that's what you're sure you want. But if you have any ideas about bugging, forget them. You'll get in trouble." He hung up abruptly.

I sighed. He'd once bugged an apartment for me without my permission. Now when I wanted him to . . .

I placed a call to Mark.

His line was busy, so I asked for Irving.

Irving was obviously relieved to hear from me, and I could understand why. I'd done something unprecedented: left the research department unattended.

I explained what had happened.

He was shocked. And grew uneasy again. "For God's sake, be careful, Brock!"

"I'm trying to."

"What about Brian?"

"He's poking around over at Mutual Claims this morning."

"Interviewing the entire board of directors, I suppose."

"Hardly. He's a good man, Irv. You were wrong to put him down as hard as you did."

"Maybe. Anyway, I'm glad he's there. Have you found Mr. Petacque?"

"Not yet." I changed the subject. I asked him about his trip to Dallas.

The trip had been uneventful. And there wasn't much doing at the office either. Joe Rothland was due in from Philadelphia later in the day. There'd been a number of telephone calls for me,

79

which Helen had switched to Irving. The market was still drifting.

"Where's Mutual Claims?"

Irving got me a quotation. Mutual Claims was down another point.

There was nothing else to discuss. I told him where I could be reached, but asked him to keep the information to himself. Then I had the call transferred to Mark, and this time Mark's line was free.

Mark sounded dispirited. Lombardi had been to see him again. Lombardi didn't seem to believe that he didn't know where Tom was, and now wanted to know where I was.

"What did you tell him?"

"That you'd gone to Phoenix for Ray Petacque's funeral."

"I wish you hadn't, Mark. Now the sheriff's office will be looking for *me.*"

"I thought it best to tell the truth, or something close to it."

"Well, what's done is done. Have you seen Daisy?"

"Yes."

"Has she heard from Tom again?"

"She said no, but I'm not sure she was telling the truth. She's scared, Brock. Mostly for Tom, I believe."

"Try again. She's our best bet. I'm not making any progress at this end."

"What about the detective from Chicago?"

I gave him a résumé of the information Quick had given me about the murders.

"Frightful," he said.

"Frightful," I agreed. I started to tell him where to reach me but decided not to, since he might have to face Lombardi again. And apparently he was too preoccupied to ask.

I hung up and returned to the balcony. I briefly considered moving to a different motel and registering under a false name, but came to the conclusion that that would only create more suspicion.

Gazing at the mountain, I asked myself why I thought that

Tom was still in the area. He might have gone to join Daisy and Jerry. He might have gone anywhere.

Iverson. Becket.

Harlow, Eames, Lombardi.

The telephone rang.

I went inside and answered it. My heart missed a beat when I heard the voice.

"I'm glad you've come," Steve Schroeder said. "How about having lunch with me today?"

I concealed my surprise. "O.K."

"Splendid. Shall I send a car for you?"

"No, I have a car."

"Splendid. How about meeting me at the uptown branch of the Arizona Club. It's in the United Bank of—"

"I know where it is."

"Splendid. I'll look forward to seeing you. Twelve-thirty?"

"Twelve-thirty'll be fine." Slowly I put the telephone back in its cradle and sat down on the bed. There were only two sources from whom he could have learned where I was staying: the sheriff's men or Ed Avery.

No, only one source. The sheriff's men wouldn't have had time to trace me.

– 17 –

The uptown branch of the Arizona Club occupies the top two floors of the United Bank of Arizona Building, on Central Avenue, the palm-lined thoroughfare that divides Phoenix into east and west.

I'd been there twice before, with Schroeder. It was his favorite luncheon spot. He was proud of the fact that he was a member and he liked the view from the south windows. From them you could see the Mutual Claims Building, a few blocks down the street. The Mutual Claims Building wasn't as tall as some of its neighbors; it had only eight stories. But it was a striking piece of architecture, with exterior walls of white stone and black glass, and Schroeder never seemed to tire of looking at it.

The headwaiter, without being asked, seated us at a table next to the south windows.

"Scotch?" Schroeder asked me.

"Fine," I said. "On the rocks."

"Chivas Regal," he told the waiter. "A double."

Here we go again, I thought.

"And for me a whiskey sour," he added.

I studied him. Instead of a necktie he was wearing a bola, a cord of braided leather slotted through a keeper of silver and turquoise. It gave him a moderately western appearance. Otherwise he looked as rumpled as ever. "How did you locate me, Steve?" I asked.

"Word gets around."

"I only came in last night."

"A friend of mine saw you checking in."

I thought back. I couldn't remember who'd been in the lobby at the time, but it was improbable that whoever had been there would have known both Schroeder and me. I didn't push, however. I was reasonably certain that he wouldn't tell me the truth.

He gazed at his building. It didn't seem to delight him as much as usual. His expression was somber.

The waiter brought our drinks.

Schroeder quit looking out the window. He sipped his drink. And this time he didn't try to be subtle. "Why did Tom disappear?" he asked.

"I don't know," I replied.

"Come off it, Brock."

"That's the truth. I don't know why Tom disappeared."

"You don't expect me to believe that."

"I'll go one step further. I don't even know that he *has* disappeared. He may turn up at the funeral tomorrow."

82

"That's unlikely."

"Is it?"

"He's hiding. The sheriff's men know he came into town Monday night. He hasn't contacted them. His father doesn't know where he is. His sister doesn't know where he is. You don't know where he is. In my book, that's hiding."

I drank some Scotch.

"Eventually he'll be found," Schroeder predicted.

"I hope so," I said.

His eyes narrowed. He seemed to be trying to read me.

I let him.

The waiter returned and we placed our orders. Schroeder went through the vintage wine routine. Then he began to look embarrassed. The country boy who was out of his element.

Watch out, I thought.

"I sometimes do dumb things," he said.

Like a fox, I thought.

"I'm impulsive."

As impulsive as a computer.

"I mean, when we were in New York—well, I mean, I told you that Ray—well, you know—that he was dishonest."

"Yes, you did."

"I'm sorry I said that. I must have got carried away."

"We all get carried away at times. But you must have had a reason for saying what you did."

He grew pink around the ears. "I was angry. Now Ray's dead, and I feel—well—guilty."

"That wouldn't change the facts, though, would it? Either he was a crook or he wasn't."

"He was my friend, Brock."

"Nevertheless."

"When I was trying to get started, when I didn't have a dime —what I mean is, he made it possible for me to get started. He and his father."

"And Tom," I reminded him.

83

"That was later."

"Not too much later. You needed financing in order to expand. If you hadn't got it from us . . ."

"I probably would have got it somewhere else. But now I'm saying the wrong thing again, aren't I? I'm sounding like I don't appreciate what you and Tom did."

"Don't apologize. We made money too. But I don't understand what you're getting at. You did tell me that Ray was a crook. Are you now trying to tell me that he wasn't?"

"Not exactly. All I'm trying to say is that Ray was my friend and I'm sorry I said what I did. I hope you'll forget it. I wouldn't want it to go any farther."

I drank some more Scotch. I would have accepted his words at face value if they'd come from anyone else. I would have accepted them from him too if he hadn't been wearing that duncelike expression. As it was, I suspected that instead of wanting me to forget what he'd said in New York, he wanted to make sure I remembered. "What did Ray do that made you think he was a crook?" I asked.

Schroeder didn't answer the question. He began a long, disjointed explanation of how he happened to meet Ray and how Ray and General Petacque were really his best friends, although of course he didn't see General Petacque very often, what with him living in Florida and all. He was still talking when the food and the wine came. He paused long enough to sample the wine and pronounce it satisfactory, then continued his story.

At first I wondered what the point was, but gradually I began to realize that he wasn't saying what he seemed to be saying. Actually, he wasn't praising Ray Petacque; he was defaming him. For woven through his account of what a good friend Ray had been and how much he'd liked him were hints that there were many qualities about Ray that he'd had to overlook. The fact that Ray was lazy, that his business judgment wasn't sound, that he lacked insight.

Eventually he stopped. He looked at my wineglass and said, "You've hardly touched your wine."

I smiled. "If I didn't know better, Steve, I'd swear you were trying to get me drunk."

His ears turned pink again, and there was a silence. It didn't last, though, for presently he said, "Ray was in New York last weekend. Did you happen to see him?"

"You asked me that at the Regency."

"Did I?"

"I didn't see him last weekend. I haven't seen him in months."

There was another silence. This one lasted longer. We finished our coffee. Finally Steve said, "You wouldn't know whether Tom is in financial difficulty, would you?"

The question startled me. "Yes, I would know. He's not. Far from it. Why do you ask?"

"Because Ray's death would be timely if he was. I mean, Ray and Blanche dying at the same time like that."

"I don't understand." I really didn't.

"Tom's son—what's his name? Jerry?—is going to inherit a lot of money. Tom would naturally have access to it."

I'd had plenty of thoughts in connection with the murders, but not that one. Yet it was a fact that since Ray and Blanche had no children of their own, their estate—or at least a large part of it—would go to other members of the family. "You probably know more about that than I do," I said.

"I do. Ray and I discussed it. The bulk of the money will go to Ray's sister and Blanche's brother and Tom's son. Ray's sister and her husband—all they have is his Army pay. And Blanche's brother—Blanche has been helping him for years. But Tom—well, Ray didn't think he needed the money, but he thought that someday the boy might."

"That doesn't mean that Tom could spend Jerry's inheritance. Or would, even if he could."

"I suppose not. You know how those things go, though."

85

I felt anger rise. Schroeder was not only discrediting Ray, he was also trying to place Tom in an unfavorable light. "I can assure you," I said, "that Tom doesn't need Jerry's money." I got up. "Thanks for the lunch. I have to be going."

Ray quickly got up too. "I hope you're not sore, Brock."

I managed to smile. "Of course not. It's always a pleasure to see you, Steve. Before I leave Phoenix I'd like to come over to your office. You know me—always following up on my recommendations."

"Sure. But I didn't know you were still recommending Mutual Claims. I thought you told all your customers to sell." He grinned. "It wasn't the best advice you've ever given."

I forced myself to smile too. "You really know how to hurt a guy. But who knows? If things look good, maybe I'll recommend that they buy again."

His grin faded. "Since you have a car, would you mind giving me a ride back to the office?"

"Not at all."

We started toward the elevator. And while we were waiting for it to come I asked, "What you told me about Ray being a crook —have you mentioned that to the detectives who are investigating the murders?"

This time the pinkish glow spread over his entire face. "Of course not! The man's dead. Whatever he did or didn't do, he isn't going to do it again. What kind of a guy do you think I am?"

The elevator came. We rode down to the ground floor. Schroeder's color returned to normal. He followed me out the back entrance to the building, into the parking lot where I'd left my car. The distance from the United Bank of Arizona Building to the Mutual Claims Building was short, and I knew that usually he walked, but now he got into the car with me and even gave me directions as to how to get there.

I let him off in front of the beautiful black and white building he was so proud of, thanked him again for the lunch and drove off.

The traffic, for Phoenix, was heavy. But compared to New York, driving was very easy. The citizens of Phoenix, I reflected, didn't know what a real traffic jam was. As a result, they probably lived at least five years longer than the citizens of more congested cities.

I went north on Central Avenue to Indian School Road and turned right. The traffic here was even lighter. I put more pressure on the gas pedal. As I approached Sixteenth Street I came up behind a delivery van that was going too slow for me. I glanced at the rear-view mirror and noticed a brown car behind mine. It was at least fifty feet away, however. I pulled out of my lane and passed the van.

At Twenty-fourth Street I stopped for a red light. The sun visor had slid out of its bracket. I fixed it and in so doing I again glanced at the mirror. The brown car was still behind mine, separated by a space of perhaps ten feet.

The light changed. I accelerated.

I didn't have cause to glance at the mirror a third time.

– 18 –

The red light on the telephone was flashing. I dialed the operator and asked whether there was a message for me.

There was. Call Mr. Barth in room 210.

I went next door and knocked.

Brian was looking pleased with himself.

He'd done as I'd suggested, he reported as he dropped into a chair: he'd applied for a job. He'd been told that Mutual Claims wasn't taking on any new employees at present, but he'd made friends with one of the girls in the personnel office. Her name was Millicent Harvey. He'd then wandered through the building. No one had tried to stop him.

"Did you know," he asked, hooking a chubby leg over the arm

of the chair, "that Mutual Claims occupies only the first five floors of the building? The other floors are leased to other tenants."

I said I knew that.

"It's no wonder the company is so profitable," he went on. "The overhead is incredibly low. Everything is computerized."

I sat down on the bed. I agreed that the way Mutual Claims was organized, relatively few employees could handle an enormous amount of billing. "But don't forget," I added, "this is only one office. There are branches. The branches employ people too."

"Yes, but not many. They're also computerized. The computers in the branches feed information directly into the computers here in Phoenix. The computers talk to one another." He grinned. "Can you imagine one computer telling another that it's wrong? Well, they do. I saw it. One computer was telling another, 'Please recheck your figures.' "

"Steve Schroeder is an expert at computer programming," I said. "That's one of the secrets of his success. You seem to have learned a lot in a short period of time."

His grin broadened. "Well, sure." He grew serious again. "Another thing I learned is that the sixth floor of the building is occupied by Jackley, Smith— the accounting firm that audits the books for Mutual Claims."

"I know that. Mutual Claims is Jackley, Smith's biggest customer. Having their offices in the same building saves running back and forth."

"Mutual Claims is Jackley, Smith's *only* customer, practically. There are a few smaller customers, but what really supports Jackley, Smith is Mutual Claims."

"How did you find that out?"

"In the lunchroom."

I remembered the lunchroom. It was located on the top floor of the building. Although it was open to the public, the only people who used it were those who worked in the building. "From the girl in the personnel office?"

"From her girlfriend. I found out about the lunchroom and

went up there around ten-thirty. Millicent was on her coffee break with another girl—Peggy Margolin. Peggy's the receptionist at Jackley, Smith. I said that I'd been to some of the other offices in the building, trying to get a job." He paused. "You were right about one thing, Brock: everyone was talking about the murders. The place was crowded, and as far as I could make out, that was the only topic of conversation."

"It's natural."

"Sure. At any rate, I applied for a job at Jackley, Smith too." I shook my head. "That wouldn't do us any good, Brian."

"I think it might. Jackley, Smith was involved in the other murder, you see."

I stared at him. "What other murder?"

"The murder of Lee Kelly. He worked for Jackley, Smith. He was shot to death three weeks ago. It could be there's a connection."

– 19 –

He hadn't been able to get many details, he said. All he knew was that a young man named Lee Kelly had been shot through the head as he got out of his car in the parking lot of the apartment building in which he lived. Kelly had been with Jackley, Smith for only a few months. Everyone felt particularly sad about the crime because Kelly had just become a father. His wife had given birth to a baby boy three days before.

"What makes you think there's a connection between that murder and the Petacques'?" I asked.

"I don't know. Possibly there isn't one. Phoenix has an exceptionally high crime rate, Peggy said. Millicent said that's because Phoenix reports crimes that other cities don't, which may be true. But what bothers me is that Mutual Claims is so chummy with the company that audits its books. And a company that large—

you'd expect them to use one of the big international accounting firms instead of a little local one."

"In a way, that's a reflection on me, Brian. I've been accepting Jackley, Smith's figures for years." Frank Jackley, as I recalled, had been a friend of Schroeder's ever since Schroeder settled in Phoenix. It seemed natural to me that when Schroeder set up Mutual Claims he'd give the accounting business to Jackley, Smith, and that the two companies would grow side by side.

"I don't mean it that way, Brock. And maybe I have a nasty mind. But the world is a jungle. Anyway, I put in an application at Jackley, Smith. The personnel director didn't offer much encouragement, but it gave me a chance to get acquainted."

I smiled. Looking at Brian, with his smooth skin and big blue eyes, you wouldn't think that he regarded the world as a jungle. "No, you're right. And it wouldn't hurt, I suppose, to talk to Kelly's widow."

He swung his leg off the arm of the chair. "Would you like me to?" he asked eagerly. "I got her address."

"I'd like *us* to. I'll go with you."

"Now?" He was already on his feet.

"Now's as good a time as any."

We left his room and went down to my car. I backed it out of its stall and turned it toward the main entrance to the motel. The motel consisted of three separate structures which formed a disconnected U. The swimming pool, outdoor dining patio and pitch-and-putt golf course were in the middle of the U. The parking stalls were on the perimeter of the three buildings. The only entrance to the complex was opposite the portico at the base of the U, where the lobby was.

We drove past the portico, paused for traffic at the gate, then swung into a westbound lane of Indian School Road. The afternoon sun made me squint. I lowered the sun visor and as I did so I glanced at the rear-view mirror.

A brown car emerged from the motel driveway. It headed west too.

For a moment nothing registered. Then something did.

I turned onto a side street, and at the next intersection onto another side street.

The brown car followed.

"I think we're going in the wrong direction," Brian said.

"I know it. But we're being tailed."

He looked over his shoulder. "The brown car?"

"Yes."

He said nothing further. I got us back to the motel and parked. We went up to my room. I wasn't frightened. I was angry. "I'm a damn fool," I said. "Schroeder invited me to lunch just so he could have me followed when I left."

"But why?"

"Who the hell knows why? He probably thinks I'll lead him to Tom."

"There were two men in that car."

"See if they're outside now."

Brian went out onto the balcony and came back. "All I can see is the roof of the car. It's there, though. About twenty yards down."

I did some thinking. "Let's wait fifteen minutes. Then I'll leave and walk around the pool to the lobby. You get *your* car and pick me up there."

We waited the fifteen minutes. I went down to the ground floor and skirted the swimming pool. A number of people were lounging on deck chairs. Most of them were elderly women. I entered the lobby, crossed it and waited by the door until Brian pulled up in his car. I jumped in and he sped off.

Presently he looked back. "It worked," he said happily.

"It worked this time," I said. "Next time it might not."

20

Open packing cases stood in a row along one wall. The sofa was piled with books. Stacks of dishes covered the shelf of the pass-through between the dining area and the kitchen.

"I'm afraid there isn't much room to sit down," she said. She made an effort to clear some space on the sofa. Several books fell to the floor.

Brian picked them up and helped her straighten the others. She thanked him with an uncertain smile. She was a pretty girl. Barely out of her teens, I judged. She was very pale, though, and there was a vagueness about her movements that was pathetic. She seemed lost.

"I really don't know what I'm doing," she said apologetically. "I've never moved a whole household before."

I took a waffle iron from one of the chairs in the dining area, put it on the table and brought the chair across the room. "Here," I said. "Sit down."

She sighed. "The men are coming with the truck day after tomorrow. I don't see how I can possibly be ready." She sat down.

"Where are you moving to?" I asked.

"Pittsburgh. That's where I come from. My parents—" She broke off. Her chin quivered. Tears came to her eyes. She swallowed. "I really don't want to go back. There's no place else, though. Mom will look after the baby, and I'll get a job."

I nodded. I felt awfully sorry for her. And apparently Brian did too. I could see it in his eyes. "I have friends in Pittsburgh," I said.

"So do I," said Brian.

The girl perked up a bit. Brian and I mentioned the names of the people we knew. They didn't mean anything to her. But a frail link was formed anyway; her uncle and one of Brian's friends worked for the same bank. We agreed that it was a small world.

Then she looked at me. "You said you wanted to ask some questions about Lee. What do you want to know?"

"Mainly, whether the police have any idea who killed him, and why."

She shook her head. "They just don't know. They keep coming around, asking me things—dumb things—like you'd think it was Lee's fault that he got killed, like *he* was the one who'd done something wrong, like he *deserved* to get killed. I mean, things like did he gamble or did he go out alone at night and what did he do in his spare time. Lee didn't *have* any spare time, Mr.—"

"Potter."

"He didn't *have* any spare time, Mr. Potter. All he ever did was go to school and go to work and do homework. The only thing he ever did—we ever did—is sometimes on Sunday afternoon we'd play tennis. He liked to play tennis. He was very good at it. But the police— that's the only reason I'll be glad to leave here. At least I won't have to answer any more dumb questions." She shook her head again and took a deep breath. "If you want to know the truth, it's my fault that Lee got killed. I told the police that, and it's true."

"Your fault?"

"Yes. If it weren't for me, he'd be alive. After he graduated last June, he wanted us to move to Los Angeles. I didn't want to go. I liked it here and I already knew the baby was on the way. I didn't want to leave. But if we'd left, Lee would still be alive."

"Mrs. Kelly," Brian said gently, "don't blame—"

"Please," she said, "don't call me that. Call me Charlotte. I don't feel like Mrs. Kelly anymore. I was Mrs. Kelly for two years. Now I'm back to what I was before, except that I have a baby." Her chin started to quiver again, but she bit her lip. "I couldn't wait to have a baby, and now that I have him I don't want him. Isn't that a terrible thing to say?"

Brian gave her a sympathetic look and started to speak, but at that point a cry came from the next room.

93

"He's awake," Charlotte said. "I can't get him on a schedule." She sighed wearily and got up. She left the room and returned presently with the infant. He was crying lustily.

Charlotte patted him and told him that he was dumb, that he didn't know when he was supposed to sleep or when he was supposed to eat, and that he was a terrible nuisance. Then she put her cheek against his head. "Poor dumb little guy."

He stopped crying, and she handed him to Brian. "Hold him while I heat a bottle." She went into the kitchen.

Brian sat down between the books and began awkwardly to rock the baby. "I'm afraid you're going to have a rough time," he told him.

The baby gurgled.

In a little while Charlotte came back with the bottle. She took her son and put the bottle to his mouth. He drank greedily. "Lee only saw him twice," she said.

"Exactly how was he killed?" I asked.

She shrugged. "All I know is what the police said." Two small furrows appeared between her eyes. "Why do you want to know? You said you're investment analysts."

"We do research," I replied. "A company we're interested in is considering buying a number of buildings here in Phoenix, including this one. But if the neighborhood isn't safe . . ." I let the sentence dangle.

"Oh, the neighborhood is safe enough. It's as safe as any. No neighborhood is really safe today. I don't know what happened. Lee had to work late. He was supposed to come to the hospital to see me, but by the time he got through working it was too late —visiting hours were over—so he came home. When he got out of the car someone shot him. No one saw it happen. Some people heard the shots, I guess. Most of them didn't pay any attention, but one man looked out of the window, the police said. He saw a man jump into a car and drive away. That's all."

Brian got up from the sofa and walked over to the window. I joined him. The apartment overlooked the parking area. The stalls were open on the sides but were covered by a sculptured roof of concrete. There were a few posts with lights on them to illuminate the area at night, but there were also bushes and shrubs along the walls which would have provided cover.

We went back to where Charlotte was feeding the baby. He'd finished a third of the bottle and was kicking with pleasure.

"What kind of work did your husband do?" I asked.

"He wasn't a CPA yet. He was getting ready to take the exam. But he was as good as any CPA. He would have passed the exam the first time—I know he would. Meanwhile, though, he was just working on figures and things." She began to ramble. To drift into the story of their meeting, their marriage and their life together. And I began to suspect that what was more important than the details of his job was the personality of Lee Kelly himself.

He'd evidently been very bright. Straight A's in high school. Valedictorian of his class. An honors student at Arizona State, where Charlotte had met him during her freshman year.

But bright in a particular way. Not flashy. Not intuitive. Rather a clear-thinking, logical, hard-working student who wrestled with problems until he found answers.

A stubborn young man, highly moral, somewhat narrow in his views, a stickler for detail. A young man who believed himself to be right and insisted on doing things his way. A young man with a strong sense of duty.

"He sounds almost old-fashioned," I observed.

"Oh, no!" Charlotte protested.

"I meant it in a complimentary way," I explained.

"Well, maybe. Would you like to see a picture of him?"

"Very much."

The baby had finished the bottle by then. She burped him and took him into the bedroom. When she came out she had a framed picture in her hand. A wedding picture.

Brian studied it with me. Lee Kelly had been tall, blond and attractive. He'd stood very straight beside his bride, regarding the camera through horn-rimmed glasses, with a smile on his lips. The carnation on his lapel was cockeyed and seemed about to fall off.

"I think I would have liked him," I said.

"I'm sure you would," Charlotte agreed.

"I imagine," Brian said, "that he would have got to the top."

"Oh, he would! They liked him a lot wherever he worked." She went on to explain that he'd been working ever since he was fourteen. He'd supported himself all the way through the university. Part-time jobs, full-time jobs—anything and everything. But he was happier at Jackley, Smith than he'd been anyplace else. Charlotte had encouraged him to remain with the firm even after he became a certified public accountant, but he'd been determined to go into business for himself. He'd had his own ideas about how things should be done.

Brian picked up on that. "He didn't approve of the way Jackley, Smith did things?"

Charlotte hesitated. "I wouldn't say that, exactly. But sometimes he thought they were kind of—I don't know—sloppy."

"Did he ever work on the Mutual Claims account?" I asked.

"Practically everybody in the company worked on the Mutual Claims account," she replied. "It's a very important account. All those hospitals and everything. That's what bothered him."

Brian frowned. So did I. "Something bothered him?" I asked.

"Last month. It had something to do with one of the hospitals —I don't know which one. But he told Mr. Jackley about it. He wanted Mr. Jackley to do something. Mr. Jackley wouldn't. That bothered Lee."

"What was wrong with the hospital?" I asked.

"I don't know. There was some kind of a discrepancy. I told him to let Mr. Jackley handle it and if Mr. Jackley thought it was all right, then it was all right. But Lee wasn't like that."

"Did he ever meet Mr. Schroeder?" I asked. "Or Mr. Ray Petacque?"

Charlotte brightened. "You know them?"

"Our company was the original underwriter of Mutual Claims."

She seemed pleased. "It really *is* a small world, isn't it? Yes, we met both of them. At the Christmas party. It was a beautiful party. I was into my ninth month, but I had a good time anyway."

"Who gave the party?" Brian asked.

"Mr. Jackley did. It was really for our people, but he invited some of the people from Mutual Claims too, they being such big customers and all."

"About the discrepancy," Brian said. "What did your husband finally do?"

"I never found out. I had the baby right after that, and, well, we didn't talk about it again. Maybe he didn't do anything. I always liked Mexicans before, but now I don't think I do."

"Mexicans?" I said.

"The man who shot Lee was a Mexican. At least that's what the police think. And they asked all these dumb questions about did we know any Mexicans. Well, we did know one at school. He was at our wedding. But it couldn't have been him. He was studying geology."

Brian bore down on that point, but with unsatisfactory results. The man who'd looked out the window after hearing the shots had told the police that he thought the man who drove off might have been a Mexican, and the police had merely been following up this lead. Charlotte, however, had latched onto it and had managed to convince herself that her husband had indeed been killed by a Mexican. "Probably a wetback."

She felt that robbery might have been a motive, although nothing had been stolen. Either the killer had been scared off before he could complete the crime or else he was just a crazy man who, if he wasn't an illegal alien, was an escapee from some mental hospital. So far the police had no suspect and they'd been honest enough to admit that such crimes, in which the victims are picked more or less at random, often go unsolved.

I asked about the gun, but she seemed to have no information on that score. She didn't think that it had been found, but she wasn't sure. The details of the crime, I guessed, simply didn't

97

matter to her. What mattered to her was the fact that her husband was dead, that she felt bereft, alone and inadequate. She was obviously having a difficult time coping with the two new roles —motherhood and widowhood—that had been thrust upon her almost simultaneously.

In time, I thought, she'd adjust. She was too young not to. Yet I wished that there was something I could do to help.

"These friends of mine in Pittsburgh," I said presently. "Why don't you call them? They're stockbrokers. If you tell them you know me, maybe they'll give you a job."

She was delighted.

So in the end I was able to do that much for her. On a memo pad I wrote a short note of introduction to Dick Atwood, a friendly competitor of mine.

And shortly after that we left.

Brian, who usually looked cheerful no matter what he was thinking, appeared troubled.

"Once she gets back to her family she'll be all right," I said.

"I hope so," he replied. "For the kid's sake." We got into the car. He started to put the key into the ignition, then paused. "At any rate, we know that Kelly wasn't the random victim of some crazy Mexican wetback."

"We don't know," I said. "We suspect. I wish we could find out more about that discrepancy he found."

"The man probably was a Mexican, though."

I glanced at him. "What makes you think so?"

"Back at the motel, when I got in my car to pick you up, I managed to get a good look at the car that had been following us. The two men were sitting in it. Both of them looked Mexican."

21

When we reached the motel we went through the same routine we'd used in leaving it, but in reverse. Brian let me off under the portico and parked the car. I walked across the inside of the U and went up to my room.

He joined me there and gave me the news that the brown car was still parked where it had been before and the two men were in it. "I don't like it," he said. "I think we ought to get out of this place."

"Possibly," I said. "But I'd rather not."

"Then call the police."

"I'd rather not do that either."

"Do you want them to go on stalking you?"

"If they'd meant to do me any harm, they'd have done it by now. But no, I don't." I thought for a moment, then went to the telephone and dialed the Mutual Claims office. I asked for Mr. Schroeder. A secretary came on the line. Mr. Schroeder was in conference, she said; could she help me? I gave her my name. Evidently it meant something to her, for she said she'd see whether Mr. Schroeder could be disturbed.

He could.

"Brock?"

"I hate to bother you, Steve, but I have a problem and I need some help."

"Of course, Brock. Anything. What's the problem?"

"When I left your office this afternoon I was followed by what looked like two Mexicans in a brown car. It's rather annoying."

There was a silence. Finally he asked, "What would you like me to do about it?"

"Well, I figure you pull a certain amount of weight in this

town. I'd appreciate your calling the police and finding out whether the two men are working for them."

"I doubt that they'd tell me that."

I glanced at Brian. He was smiling. I winked at him. "Then perhaps I'd better call the police myself."

There was another silence. "O.K. Brock, I'll see what I can do. I can't guarantee results, though."

"I understand that. But I'd appreciate the effort. I'll see you tomorrow."

"Any word from Tom?"

I didn't answer. I simply hung up.

"You think it'll work?" Brian asked.

"I wasn't sure before, but I am now. It will."

"Why did he do it, though?"

"Because he's anxious as hell to locate Tom. What I don't understand is how he found out I'm staying here. All I can think of is that Ed Avery told him."

"But Mr. Avery is Mr. Petacque's friend, you said."

"I know. I really believe he is. Yet . . ." I was out of explanations.

"What are you going to do now?"

"I'm stumped. Tom has other friends here. Originally I thought I'd start with Ed and go down the list. But now it seems kind of hopeless. Possibly Tom's wife knows where he is and Mark can find out from her. Otherwise we'll just have to wait. Sooner or later he'll turn up."

"I wish there was something I could do to help."

"You've already done quite a bit, Brian. But there is one thing. You can get the license number of that brown car and take a good look at the two men."

"I already did that." He gave me the license number. "I'm not sure about the faces," he added. "It would've been easier if there were only one man. I did the best I could, though."

I smiled as I wrote down the license number. "Your best is pretty good."

He shrugged. And mentally left me. A faraway look came into his eyes.

My thoughts began to wander also. The energy and optimism with which I'd started the day was ebbing. I hadn't accomplished anything. Whatever information we had was the result of Brian's efforts. And even that—what did it add up to? A young employee of Jackley, Smith had been murdered. Possibly he'd been murdered as a result of something he'd learned about Mutual Claims. But possibly he hadn't.

I walked over to the glass door that led to the balcony. The late afternoon sun cast a purple shadow across the mountain. Gazing at it, I had the feeling that I was a long way from home, in a place where I wasn't well acquainted, on a mission that I didn't know how to handle.

Mark was right: I was good at getting information. Financial information. I knew how to interpret figures and interview the people who'd prepared them. But that was a different kind of work. I was in no way prepared to track down a man who, for one reason or another, didn't want to be found.

My thoughts grew even darker. Suppose Tom was dead.

I turned away from the glass door and its view of the mountain, which suddenly seemed sinister.

Brian was sitting on the bed, again wearing a troubled look.

"What are you thinking about?" I asked.

"The baby," he replied.

The last thing I would have guessed.

"It isn't good for a kid to be unwanted," he added. "I know."

"He's wanted," I said.

"I hope so."

I sat down on a chair. There were more sides to Brian's personality than I'd imagined. There was even a vulnerable side.

The troubled look disappeared. "What are we going to do next?" he asked.

"Nothing," I said.

He seemed disappointed.

"Absolutely nothing."

"Because you think . . . ?"

"Because I don't know what to think. Because I don't know what to do. Because I came out here with the crazy idea that Tom would be easy to find, that all I'd have to do was contact Ed Avery, and it isn't working out that way. Because I'm not even sure at this moment that Tom's alive."

"He's alive."

"What makes you say that?"

"I just think so. I haven't been around him as much as I've been around you and I don't know him as well as you do, but I have the feeling that no matter what kind of ups and downs he has, he's really not the victim type."

You haven't seen him in the condition in which I've seen him, I thought. But I recalled what Dr. Balter had said: Tom wasn't the kind of person to take his hostilities out on himself. Which was another way of saying what Brian had said. If one could believe that all victims contributed to their own victimization. "Perhaps," I said dubiously. "In any event, I don't know what to do. And when that happens, I've found, it's generally best not to do anything."

"If you say so." He didn't sound convinced.

I was beginning to feel better, though. "Besides, we may have done enough already."

He eyed me skeptically.

But as it turned out I was right. We had done enough already.

For twenty minutes later Ed Avery telephoned. With the information that Tom wanted to see me.

– 22 –

He refused to tell me over the telephone where Tom was. He insisted on meeting me someplace other than his house and accompanying me. He suggested the lobby of Camelback Inn. I agreed.

It hadn't occurred to me until then that my telephone might be bugged. I still didn't think that it was. Nevertheless I approved of Ed's caution and decided to be extra careful myself. I asked Brian to see whether the brown car was still parked where it had been before. He reported that it was. I gave him directions on how to get to the Arizona Biltmore and told him to wait for me there, in the lobby. I drove my car to the airport.

The brown car followed me.

I took the rental contract out of the glove compartment, gave the car to the attendant, hurried into the airport and out through a door on the other side. I walked quickly to the taxi rank, got into the first cab and told the driver to take me to the Arizona Biltmore.

The taxi wasn't followed.

Brian was standing by the registration desk. I gave him the rental contract and instructions to take a taxi back to the airport, pay for my car, rent another one for himself from a different agency, drive back to our motel and stay in his room until he heard from me.

I drove his car to Camelback Inn.

Ed was sitting on the edge of a chair, smoking a cigarillo, watching the door. He jumped up when he saw me and strode across the lobby. "It took you long enough."

"I had to get rid of the men who were following me," I explained.

He threw a swift glance over my shoulder toward the door. Ash fell from his cigarillo. He didn't notice it. He lowered his voice. "You were followed?"

"Partway. I got rid of them."

"By who?"

"Two Mexicans, they looked like. On Schroeder's orders, I believe."

He took my arm and led me outside. We went a short distance along a walk toward one of the swimming pools. "I want to know about it," he said.

I extricated myself from his grip, which was hurting me. "Did you tell Schroeder where I was staying?"

"I haven't talked to Schroeder in three months." He dropped what was left of the cigarillo onto the concrete and ground it out with the toe of his boot. "Can't stand the man."

"Well, somebody did. He called me at the motel after I got back from your place and invited me to lunch. When I left him I was followed. You were the only one who knew where I was."

Deep furrows appeared between his eyes. "You weren't followed earlier?"

"I don't think so."

The furrows grew even deeper. "You might have been. By Armand Petacque."

I hadn't thought of that.

"He sure as hell wants to find Tom. He called this afternoon on the telephone. He'd changed his tune. He was practically begging. He said he was convinced I knew where Tom is. I finally had to hang up on him."

"Where is Tom?"

He hesitated, and for a moment I thought he'd changed his mind about taking me. But then he said, "At the Franciscan Renewal Center."

"The what?"

"It's only a few miles from here. It's a retreat."

"I'll be damned. I wish you'd told me this morning. It would've saved a day."

"I thought I ought to get his permission first. And that took some doing." His fingers closed around my arm again. He led me farther along the walk, toward the pool. "He's in bad shape, Brock. I don't know what to do. He practically saw the murders."

I stopped, forcing him to stop also. "He . . . what?"

Ed simply nodded.

"And he hasn't told the police?"

He shook his head. "I'd like him to, but he's almost a basket case."

"For God's sake, man, withholding information like that is a crime!"

"I know."

"And you're as guilty as he is."

"I know that too."

I was speechless.

He walked on, pulling me with him. We reached the glass-enclosed pool area. An attendant was rolling up plastic mattresses and putting them away. A bald-headed man in a terry-cloth bathrobe was asleep in a deck chair, his sunglasses dangling from one ear. No one else was around. "I don't care so much about myself," Ed continued. "I'm older than I look, and I've had a pretty good run for my money—longer than I thought I'd have when they took out that lung. And it's been years since there was anyone I was important to. But I'm worried about Tom."

I tried to apply reason to the situation, but my mind balked. "You shouldn't smoke," I said.

"I don't usually," he said. "But the past couple of days have been . . . hellish. I don't care about many people in this here world anymore, but I do care about Tom. Have, ever since he was a kid. A damn sight more than his father did."

My mind went back into action. "You've let your feelings cloud your judgment. You've got to make him go to the police. The three of us'll go if necessary."

"Don't say that. You haven't seen him yet."

"I don't care what shape he's in—he's going to the police."

105

Ed turned away. He gazed beyond the pool, beyond the grounds of the hotel, at the distant mountains. "It's a nice valley," he said presently. "It was even nicer in the old days, before it got all cluttered up with people." He paused, and gestured with his head. "Ray's house is right over there."

I looked in the direction he'd indicated. The sun had set, but the sky wasn't yet dark. The distant mountains were black, like smoke, but the nearer ones were amethyst, and you could see the houses that dotted their lower slopes. They were expensive houses.

"Paradise Valley," Ed mused. "They named it right. But it was better before. Now there's too much money. Much too much. Most of it made back East."

"About Tom," I said, to bring his thoughts back from where they were.

But he wasn't ready to let them come back. "Where Ray's house is, I used to ride my pony. Shot a coyote once, just about where his tennis court is." He sighed. "Never did like coyotes."

"But about Tom. He practically saw the murders, you said."

"Called my pony Hoho. Short for Hohokam. Old Indian tribe. Lived here a thousand years ago." He sighed again and turned back to me. "Tom? That's what he says. At first I didn't believe him—I didn't believe there'd been any murders—but now I know he really did."

The man who'd been asleep in the deck chair woke up. He stretched and looked around, momentarily bewildered. Then he took off his sunglasses, got to his feet, pulled his bathrobe tight and hurried past us toward the hotel.

Ed waited until the man was out of earshot before continuing. "He got here Monday evening. Rented a car at the airport. He was going to drive Ray and Blanche somewhere. One time he says Los Angeles, another time Albuquerque, another time Mexico—the fact of the matter is, I think, he hadn't made up his mind where he was going to take them. But Ray was in some sort of trouble, and Tom was trying to help. He wanted to get him and

106

Blanche away someplace where nobody knew where they were, until Ray could sort things out and decide what to do. He had an idea that if he drove them in a car that was rented in his name rather than theirs, stashed them in some motel, then brought the car back to where he'd got it, no one would be able to trace them. It might have worked too, but evidently he got to the house just a few minutes too late."

"What happened?"

"It was dark by the time he got there. He had his headlights on. He pulled into the driveway. You know how the house is laid out, with the big turn-around driveway and the garage on the side, facing the street, and a door leading from the garage into the laundry room?"

"I don't remember. All I remember is a sprawling place with a swimming pool and tennis court in back."

"Well, that's the layout. Anyway, there was another car parked in the driveway by the front door. Tom stopped. The garage door was open, and apparently the headlights from his car were shining right into the garage. He saw two men carrying Ray into the garage from the laundry room. It must have been a terrible sight, enough to shake the hell out of anyone, and it's stuck in Tom's mind, and he can't get rid of it. He says they were carrying Ray like he was a sandbag, one at each end. Ray's head was hanging to one side at a weird angle, and there was blood on him. I don't know what Tom did—he himself doesn't seem to know—but apparently he opened the door of his car and started to get out, but at that moment the men saw the light, and one of them dropped Ray—the one who was supporting his head—and pulled out a gun and fired at Tom. Tom keeps talking about Ray's head hitting the floor, as if he wasn't dead and could feel it. At any rate, my guess is that the man was blinded by the headlights and the shot missed. But there's a nick at the edge of the car door. Tom has no recollection of driving away, other than a hazy recollection that he hit something, or of deciding to come to my house, and I can believe it—he was a wreck when he got there."

"I can imagine."

"He did hit something, I think. The mailbox in front of the house. I went over there the next day. The post with the mailbox on it was cockeyed, and there were tire marks on the lawn which probably were made by Tom's car."

"You should have taken him straight to the police."

"For Christ's sake, Brock, I wish you'd quit telling me what I should have done! I had a man on my hands who was coming apart at every seam. He wasn't even coherent most of the time. He kept talking about how he hadn't loved his brother and how his brother's head hit the floor and all kinds of crazy things. It's taken me three days to get enough sense out of him to put together the story."

"So what did you do?"

"I gave him a drink. I thought it would calm him. Instead it made him throw up. Finally I fixed some hot tea. That worked. He kept it down, and I gave him a sleeping pill to go with it. He fell asleep sitting in a chair."

"The poor son of a bitch."

"I sat up all night, afraid to leave him alone in case he might wake up and try to leave. I tried to figure out what he'd been talking about. Two men carrying Ray into the garage, someone taking a shot at *him*—I couldn't imagine any of it really happening, yet I wasn't sure. As soon as the newspaper came, I brought it in and read it. There was no mention of Ray. Then I turned on the television. Same there. But when Tom woke up he started all over again. I told him I thought he ought to see a doctor. That made him worse—he tried to run away; I actually had to restrain him physically; it was damn hairy for a few minutes. Then I thought of the retreat. It's not meant for people who are in the shape Tom was in—it's for something else altogether—but one of the priests is a friend of mine. I've given donations from time to time. I promised Tom I'd go over to Ray's house myself and look around if he'd let me take him to the retreat. It worked." He groaned. "What a night!"

I pictured Ed's house. I pictured Tom asleep in a chair. I pictured Ed grappling with him.

"Anyway," he continued, "I got him to the Renewal Center and settled down, then just to satisfy myself I went over to Ray's house. The front door was locked. The garage doors were closed. Except for the fact that the mailbox was cockeyed, there was no sign that anything was wrong. I went home and called a doctor friend of mine. I thought I'd give Tom a day or two to rest, then get him to the doctor's office. But yesterday morning when I brought in the newspaper and saw the headline—well, I realized."

The pool attendant had finished his chores and left. We were alone. I said nothing. I really couldn't fault Ed. He'd done a lot. Almost too much.

He turned away again. "Too many people," he said. "Too much money. It was better before."

"Come on," I said. "Let's go. I'm anxious to see Tom."

"You're sure you weren't followed?"

"Positive."

We walked across to the parking lot and got into his car.

– 23 –

A compound of rambling white buildings with a parking lot in front. Except for the cross, it looked like a guest ranch.

The sound of singing greeted us. A hymn, offered with enthusiasm.

"You wait here," Ed told me as we entered the lobby. "I'll see what kind of mood he's in."

"He knows I'm coming, doesn't he?"

"Even so."

He crossed the lobby and went out into a courtyard. I strolled over to a doorway marked "CHAPEL."

The room was filled. A man in a green sport shirt was perched on a tall stool at one side of the altar, strumming a guitar, but the voices of the singers were so loud that you couldn't hear the instrument. The hymn was one I was unfamiliar with. It had to do with freeing the spirit.

A woman in the back row noticed me. She gave me an ecstatic smile and motioned for me to come in. I shook my head.

The hymn ended. I backed out of the doorway. The woman who'd noticed me left her seat and came after me.

"Do come in and join us," she said. Her expression was one of utter bliss.

"Thank you," I said, "but I'm just visiting."

"Visitors are welcome. On this earth we're all visitors."

"Maybe later. Not right now."

She regarded me for a moment with what appeared to be consuming love, then said, "Well, make yourself at home. Be happy. Bless you." And hurried back to the chapel.

There were some pamphlets on a table. I picked up one of them. It listed the encounter groups that were available at the center. Weekend marathons, couples therapy groups, groups for professional people and a special introductory course dealing with ego states, stroking and the games people play. They were designed, the pamphlet said, to improve your self-image, heighten your awareness and make you more genuine.

Ed returned. "He's O.K.," he said. "More or less. Come on."

We walked across the courtyard. There were buildings with sleeping rooms on each side and a swimming pool at the far end. Ed guided me toward the building on the left and along its sheltered terrace. The doors to the rooms had plaques on them which stated who'd donated them. Tom's was at the very end of the building. It was ajar.

He was sitting on the bed, his elbows on his knees, staring at the floor. He looked up as we entered. "Brock," he said with an attempt at a smile.

I sat down beside him and put my arm around his shoulder. I

had varied emotions, but a feeling of relief predominated. I said, "What the hell, fella, it's not all that bad."

"I'm sorry," he said. "I've caused everybody so much trouble. Ray's dead. They killed him."

"I know."

"I didn't get there in time. Do you think it's my fault?"

"Of course not."

"I never liked him the way I should have."

"You liked him as much as you could."

"He was my brother."

I wondered whether he knew that Blanche also was dead.

He did, for his next words were, "They killed Blanche too, Ed says. Do you think it's my fault?"

"No."

"I hope Daisy's all right. I'm worried about her and Jerry."

"They're all right." I glanced at Ed. He was wearing a see-what-I-mean expression.

"I caused everybody a lot of trouble," Tom said.

I had a sudden hunch that sympathy might not be the best approach. I removed my arm from his shoulder and stood up. I planted myself in front of him. "You certainly did. Mainly by not trusting Mark and me, by trying to handle things yourself. You sold us short, and that was stupid."

He gave me a startled look. "I'm sorry."

"Being sorry isn't going to do any good. Being sorry is a cop-out. And sitting there on that bed, feeling guilty, is a cop-out too. What the fuck do you expect to do—sit there for the rest of your life, hating yourself for something that isn't even your fault? Well, I'll be goddamned if I'm going to let you. You're going to get off your ass and start making sense."

He blinked, and his jaw went slack. "I'm sorry."

"I just got through telling you that being sorry isn't going to do any good. What you have to do is *do* something."

"I thought you liked me."

111

"I don't give a shit what you thought or what you think. I do like you, when you make sense. I don't like you when you're the way you are now." I felt a tug on my sleeve. Ed apparently thought I was being too rough. I ignored it. "I didn't fly three-quarters of the way across the country because I don't like you. But now that I'm here, seeing you stare at the floor and not do anything, I wonder whether I really should have."

"Take it easy," Ed said in a low voice.

I swung around and said, "Bullshit." By pretending to be angry I'd actually become angry. "Stand up," I told Tim.

He didn't move.

"Stand up, goddamn it!"

He got slowly to his feet.

"That's better. Now tell me what you and Ray had a fight about last Saturday night."

He sat down again.

I took him by the arms and pulled him up. He let me. And this time he remained standing. "Saturday night," I said. "What was it all about?"

"Ray said he killed a man."

My anger evaporated. "I don't believe it. Who?"

"A man named Lee Kelly."

I gaped at him. "Ray killed Lee Kelly?"

"Not himself. Someone else did. But Ray agreed to it. Ray started the whole thing." Something new came into his eyes: curiosity. "You knew Lee Kelly?"

"I met his widow this afternoon."

And the transformation began at that point. Nothing I'd said before had caused much of a change in his manner. But the fact that I'd met Lee Kelly's widow had a profound effect. It was as if for the first time he realized that someone shared his problem —and I could only guess at how desperately alone with it he must have been feeling. His shoulders went back, his chin went up, even his color began to change—his face became less gray.

It didn't happen all at once, but it did happen quickly, and

112

while he didn't suddenly flex his muscles and cry, "I feel wonderful!" he obviously was finding new strength and seemed to be aware of it.

So much so that Ed muttered, "Well, I'll be damned."

"How did you meet her?" Tom asked.

"Brian heard about the murder and thought there might be a connection between that one and Ray's."

"Brian Barth?"

"Yes."

"He's here too?"

"I brought him along to help."

He smiled, and this time it was more than an attempt. "You're quite a guy."

"Getting back to last Saturday night," I said.

The smile left his face. I was afraid he was going to lapse into apathy again, but he didn't. "I didn't know Ray was coming into town," he said. "He called from the airport. He said he had to see me right away. He sounded upset. I told him, 'All right, come on over.' "

It must have been a strange scene, I thought as I listened to his account of what took place between them after dinner. Emotionally, like a seesaw—Ray down, Tom up; Tom down, Ray up. Of the two, Tom had always been the more volatile, but on this occasion he wasn't. At least at the beginning. However, as Ray unburdened himself of the events in Phoenix he calmed down, and Tom grew excited. Then, after making wild accusations of negligence and indifference, Tom cooled off and Ray got angry.

The trouble had started at the Christmas party given by Jackley, Smith, Ray claimed.

A young man whom he didn't even know came up to him and introduced himself as Lee Kelly. He worked for Jackley, Smith, he said, and he hoped that Ray had a few minutes to discuss a problem. Ray said, "Sure," and Kelly explained that he was a member of the team that was preparing the figures for the annual closing of the Mutual Claims books. He'd discovered what he thought was a mistake. It concerned Angelica Hospital in Sarasota, Florida. "I know the hospital," Ray said. "My father lives in Sarasota." That was a coincidence, Kelly said, because while he wasn't from Sarasota himself, he'd once been there and been treated at Angelica Hospital for a severe case of sunburn. Then Kelly asked whether in Ray's opinion a little hospital like that could handle two hundred thousand outpatient visits per year. Ray said that two hundred thousand seemed very high. Kelly said that it seemed more than very high; it seemed impossible. "But that's what our records show," he added. "I told Mr. Jackley about it, and he said, 'Nothing of the kind.' " Ray replied that someone had probably made a mistake. He suggested that Kelly check the figures again and let him know if he found any other mistakes, and dismissed the conversation from his mind.

Three days later Kelly called him on the telephone to report that he'd found five more instances where the number of outpatient visits seemed exceptionally large for the size of the hospital. Ray said he'd look into the matter, and mentioned it to Schroeder.

Schroeder was evasive. Ray persisted. Schroeder lost his temper. Ray backed off.

But the following morning Schroeder brought the subject up himself. He'd inquired about Lee Kelly, he said. "He's nothing but a troublemaker. He ought to be removed from the scene." To which Ray replied, "If that's the case, I couldn't agree more."

And within thirty-six hours Kelly was dead.

Ray had been brooding ever since.

"Ray was a strange guy," Tom said. "I never really understood him. I never thought he had much conscience. As far as he was concerned, I thought, the whole world could fall apart and as long as he personally wasn't inconvenienced he wouldn't care. But I guess there was another side to him."

"There wasn't," Ed stated with conviction.

"Well, in this case I think there was. He wouldn't let the matter rest. He began to bug people around the office. He even

114

went to Frank Jackley. He tried to get at the facts. No one would tell him anything. For the first time, I think, he began to realize how unimportant he was in the company. He must have made quite a nuisance of himself. Finally Schroeder told him so, told him he was making a nuisance of himself. He blew up. He told Schroeder that between him and Dad they owned as much stock in the company as Schroeder did, and that he was an officer, and that he wanted to know what was going on. Schroeder laughed at him. That made him even madder. He lost his head and accused Schroeder of ordering Kelly's murder. Schroeder denied it, of course. In no uncertain terms. But then he said an odd thing. He said that if he *had* ordered Kelly's murder, then Ray was as guilty as he was, because Ray had agreed to it. And when Ray thought about it he realized that he had. If there'd been a conspiracy, he was part of it. He hadn't thought Kelly would be killed, naturally—he'd thought, simply, that he'd be fired. But now he was scared. And I began to get scared too. Not because I thought Ray would ever be convicted of conspiracy to commit a murder, but because the company is crooked."

"What evidence do you have of that?" I asked.

"None," Ed said flatly.

"Not much," Tom agreed. "Ray never was able to find out very much. But he found out enough to convince him that the records are wrong, that some of the hospitals don't treat as many outpatients as Mutual Claims says they do. And now, of course, Ray is dead. That's evidence of something, wouldn't you say?"

"Not necessarily," Ed pointed out.

I wished that he'd quit throwing in his opinions. "You think Mutual Claims is overcharging the hospitals?" I asked Tom.

He shook his head.

"I don't either," I said.

"Why not?" Ed asked.

"Because it isn't possible," I said. "Even though the hospitals have their outpatient billing done by an outside company, they have a general idea of how many outpatients they treat. Sooner

115

or later they'd realize they were being charged for patients they weren't treating. And sooner, rather then later."

"That's true," he admitted.

Tom and I exchanged a glance. It said that we were on the same wavelength. And I could understand the anxiety that had driven him to the brink of a nervous breakdown. I began to share it. My feelings must have communicated themselves to him, for he sank down on the bed again and began to look morose. "It's bad," he said. "Poor Ray. Poor Blanche."

"Cut that out," I said. "Go on with what happened."

And after a few moments he did.

He'd accused Ray, he said, of sitting back and letting Schroeder run the business to suit himself, of being lazy and irresponsible. Ray at first had tried to justify himself but had ended by becoming angry. They parted on bad terms, with nothing resolved. Then Tom began to think about the implications of what Ray had told him—the implications not only for Ray but for all of us. He saw Price, Potter and Petacque losing its license. He saw our individual reputations ruined. He imagined lawsuits, even jail sentences. He began to feel despondent.

"Where did you get the gun?" I asked.

He blinked. "Daisy told you about that?"

"Yes."

"It wasn't my gun. It was Ray's. I took it away from him. He'd been carrying it around for a week. He was afraid that someone might try to do to him what they'd done to Lee Kelly. But then when he got excited he began waving it at me. I talked him into handing it over."

I had a sudden desire to laugh. It was all I could do to restrain myself.

"She hid it," he went on. "In the same place she hides everything. I found it. I threw it away Monday morning on the way to the office. Did you think . . . ? No, you couldn't." He reflected. "Well, maybe you were right. I don't know. I can't remember all the things that went through my mind. I guess I did want to die. But it wasn't like—well, I don't know. Don't ask me questions I can't answer."

I began to see everything in a brighter light. But at the same time I began to wonder.

"Anyway," Tom said, "I was sorry for some of the things I'd said to Ray. I called him on Sunday. We kind of half made up. I told him to go back to Phoenix. I said I'd come out on Monday and take him and Blanche away somewhere. He needed time, I thought, to put things together. Meanwhile I intended to have a talk with Schroeder. Between Ray and me, I thought, maybe we could get to the bottom of things. But first I had to protect you and Mark if I could."

"It was too late," I said.

"I realize that now." He paused. "It was too late for everything. When I got to Phoenix I drove to Ray's house . . . Did Ed tell you?"

I nodded.

"Well, then you know. I guess I flipped. I don't know what I'd have done if it weren't for Ed."

"You were in bad shape, all right," Ed assured him.

"What hotel was Ray staying at in New York?" I asked.

He told me. It was a small hotel on lower Park Avenue. I'd heard of the place but had never been there. "Why?" he asked.

"Just curious," I said. "I tried to locate him at the Park Lane and couldn't."

"That's why he didn't go there. He was afraid someone might try to locate him."

"Why did you tell Daisy she and Jerry are in danger?"

"That was my idea," Ed said quickly. "I think they might be."

I looked at him. "Why?"

"Someone might try to use them to get at Tom."

It was possible, I supposed. Anything was possible. I turned

117

back to Tom. "You're going to have to tell your story to the police."

There was a long silence. Tom's face darkened. The muscles of his jaw began to pulse. "How can I?" he asked hopelessly.

Ed tugged at my sleeve. I moved closer to him. "I don't think he's up to it yet," he said in a low voice.

"You can't hide here indefinitely," I told Tom. "I don't even think you want to."

"But, Brock, what about us?"

"Don't tell them about Schroeder. Don't tell them anything Ray said. Tell them you were having an anxiety attack. Tell them Ray saw you in New York and got worried. He persuaded you to come out to Phoenix and go away with him for a little while. But tell them everything else just as it happened."

He considered. "And you?"

"I'll do what I can."

"Have you got any of your pills?" Tom asked Ed.

Ed reached into his pocket and came up with two pills.

"Wait a minute," I said. "What are those?"

"Nembutal," he said.

"He's been bringing them to me," Tom explained. "They've helped. At least I slept."

"Just two a day," Ed added. "It was the only thing I could think of."

I took the pills and looked them over.

"Believe me," Ed said.

"I believe you," I said finally. "Under the circumstances, maybe it's a good idea." I handed the pills to Tom. "Take both of them."

He did, and by the time we got him to the sheriff's office he was barely awake.

– 24 –

They interrogated all of us. First Ed, then me, and finally Tom. They didn't call it "interrogating"; they called it "interviewing." They're touchy about their image, one of the detectives explained, and "interviewing" sounds better.

It wasn't as bad as I expected, at least where Ed and I were concerned. There was a lot of waiting around. There was a certain amount of kibitzing. They wouldn't let us leave, yet they didn't seem to know what to do with us. So we sat there in the Mesa substation, first in an office that no one was using at the moment, then, as they got used to us, wherever we felt like sitting. We looked at maps of the area covered by the Mesa unit. We inspected the electronic equipment that linked the substation with the patrol cars, with downtown headquarters and with other law-enforcement agencies. They let us listen to reports coming in from various cars and showed us the rifles that they kept in a rack outside the lieutenant's office. We drank Pepsi-Cola from a vending machine, which made for even more sociability, since no one had change for a dollar and we were borrowing quarters and dimes from one another. I smoked cigarettes until I ran out of them, and Ed discovered that he had a hole in one of his socks.

As far as Tom was concerned, it was a different matter, however. Exactly what was going on, I didn't know, for they had him in an office with the door closed. But every now and then one of the detectives would come out to say something to one of the other officers, and I gathered that the main problem was keeping Tom coherent. They brought him Pepsi-Cola and coffee and were managing, it appeared, to extract from him a story of sorts, but the process was a slow one. Both Ed and I had explained Tom's condition, and Ed had taken the blame for the sleeping pills, which seemed to trouble them almost as much as the murders.

But since it was a murder case they were investigating, not a narcotics case, and since Ed indignantly offered to get his doctor to swear that he'd given him a prescription for the pills, they didn't seem to be about to make an issue over them. And the pills evidently were serving their purpose, giving Tom a certain credibility as a man who'd been distraught to begin with and whose state of mind had deteriorated further as a result of what he'd seen at his brother's house. I supplied the detectives with Dr. Balter's name and suggested that they contact him. Ed gave them the name of the priest with whom he'd made arrangements for Tom to enter the Renewal Center. The detectives thought it peculiar that he'd chosen to take Tom there rather than to a hospital, but Ed insisted that he had great faith in the healing powers of meditation and rest.

More important than what we told them, of course, was what we didn't tell them. Neither Ed nor I said a thing about Mutual Claims or Lee Kelly or the two men who had followed me during the afternoon. We had no way of knowing what Tom was telling them, and I was afraid that under the influence of the barbiturate he might spill the whole story. There was nothing I could do about that, however, so I simply hoped for the best.

Along about one o'clock in the morning I thought of calling Brian to tell him where I was, and it was a good thing I did, for he said he'd been worried.

Shortly after three o'clock Harlow informed Ed and me that we could go, provided we'd come back later to sign formal statements and provided I didn't try to leave Phoenix. I said we'd wait for Tom. He said it might be a long wait. I said we'd wait anyway.

I slept for a few minutes, sitting in a chair. I went out to buy cigarettes, but couldn't find a store that was open. I drank some more Pepsi-Cola and watched dawn break. Some of the officers who'd been on duty during the night went home, and others arrived. I didn't try to get acquainted with anyone on the new shift, and neither did Ed—he was asleep with his head on one of the desks. I began to feel as if I'd lived my entire life in the Mesa substation of the Maricopa County Sheriff's office.

And at half-past eight they released Tom. They made it clear that the release was conditional. They would want to question him again, possibly within a matter of hours. They did not want him to leave the city. They wanted to inspect the car he'd been driving, which Ed told them was parked in the garage of neighbors of his who were vacationing. They wanted a signed statement.

But they did not, it seemed, suspect him of murdering his brother and sister-in-law. At least not yet.

Tom's face was the color of milk, and he was very subdued. He was ready to agree to anything, just to get out of the place. And he was still groggy, although the worst effects of the Nembutal had worn off.

Outside the building, Ed and I discussed what to do with him, while he stood by passively. Ed argued for taking him back to the Renewal Center. I objected. He'd be better off at the motel with me, I said. And I won. Which meant that I had to go back to the sheriff's office and give them his new address. Then we went to breakfast at the nearest restaurant we could find, for I was starved. Tom managed to get down some toast and coffee, and Ed didn't appear to be hungry either, but I had bacon and eggs and hashed brown potatoes and toast—my toast, some of Ed's and some of Tom's.

It was almost ten o'clock when we reached the motel. Ed offered to drive me over to pick up my car, which was still parked at Camelback Inn, but I said I'd get it later. I told him I was planning to attend the funeral and asked him to take me there. He said he didn't intend to go. I prevailed upon him to do so anyway. He hurried home to shave and change clothes. He'd be back in twenty minutes, he said. I took Tom up to my room and suggested he lie down. He did, and fell asleep immediately. I knocked on Brian's door and asked him to stay with Tom until I returned.

I shaved, showered, put on a clean shirt and went downstairs to wait for Ed.

Almost as an afterthought, I decided to check on the brown car.

It wasn't there.

– 25 –

Ed and I arrived after the service had started.

With all the lilies, the church looked as it might on Easter. And the crowd was of Easter proportions. I was amazed.

We couldn't find two seats together, so Ed went one way and I the other. I wound up in next to the back row, beside a carefully coiffed woman who kept fingering the aquamarine that hung from a gold chain around her neck. The stone must have weighed at least eighty karats. But the woman beyond her, who was young, represented the other end of the economic ladder—she was wearing black cotton slacks and an inexpensive white blouse that was slightly torn at the shoulder.

I was almost drunk from lack of sleep, and my mind went off in a strange direction. I found myself wondering what had brought those two women to the same church pew, to the same funeral; and why the crowd was so large. For Ray Petacque hadn't really been an important man, and Blanche Petacque hadn't been an important woman. His career in the Army had been unspectacular. He'd retired with a reasonable pension and limited prospects. He'd settled in Phoenix, mainly because of the climate and the opportunities to play tennis. Then he'd lent money to Steve Schroeder, who'd been even less important in the scheme of things than he—and had suddenly become rich. Blanche had then begun giving parties for a lot of people she didn't know very well, and—presto—here they were, half a dozen years later, mourned by hundreds. What did any of these people actually know of Ray and Blanche Petacque?

Only one person had tried to help them, and he wasn't even here. He was asleep on the bed of my motel room, half wrecked by the effort.

I looked around for Schroeder. I didn't see him. I guessed that he was somewhere up at the front of the church, along with those who supposedly had been closest to the deceased.

Mutual Claims. That was where many of these people came from. Schroeder had probably given them time off, perhaps even closed the company for the day.

And most of the Jackley, Smith crew was undoubtedly here also.

At the end of the service I filed out with the rest of the crowd. I tried to find Ed but couldn't. I headed for the parking lot, which was in back of the church. People were moving toward their cars, and some cars were lining up for the procession to the cemetery. I passed the two hearses and the limousines behind them. General Petacque was seated stiffly in the back seat of the first limousine. He saw me. He appeared to want to speak to me. I paused. For one long moment we looked at each other through the closed window. Then he changed his mind and turned away. I walked on, reached Ed's station wagon and waited. Presently I saw him coming across the pavement.

"You aren't planning to go to the cemetery, I hope," he said as he opened the door.

"No," I said.

"Did you see Schroeder?"

"No. Did you?"

"Yes. You'd think he'd lost his best friend." He put the key in the ignition and started the engine. "He looks lousy, in my opinion. Worried as hell. Want me to take you to your car?"

"I suppose."

He tried to back the wagon out of its stall, but traffic in the

123

parking lot was snarled. The cars that were in line for the procession were blocking the exit. I saw the woman with the aquamarine. She was behind the wheel of an Eldorado. There was no room for her to maneuver her car either, and she was impatiently fingering the stone that hung on the gold chain, as she'd been doing inside the church. Ed shoved the gear lever into Park and folded his arms across his chest. He looked quite different in a suit and tie, I thought. More like a businessman.

"What are you going to do now?" he asked presently.

"Get some sleep. I'm beat."

"And after that?"

"I'll have to give it some thought." By way of changing the subject, I pointed to the woman in the Eldorado and asked Ed whether he knew who she was.

"Muriel Decatur," he replied. "You remember her?"

"No. Should I?"

"She was at the housewarming party Ray and Blanche gave. I thought maybe you met her."

The cars began to move. Ed waited for an opening, then backed the wagon out of the stall and guided it toward the exit.

During the fifteen-minute drive to Camelback Inn he rambled on about Muriel Decatur. She was old Phoenix, he said. Her father had owned a dry-goods company in the days when the city was small. He'd later made a lot of money in real estate. She'd inherited a fortune. She'd also received a large divorce settlement from her husband, who'd made even more money than her father. Her ex-husband was one of the men who'd developed and promoted Scottsdale.

"Everybody out here seems to have made money in real estate," I observed.

"If they were here at the right time," he agreed, "it was hard not to. Like Los Angeles or Houston or Vegas. Just about anything you owned went up in value. It bred a bunch of optimists."

"That's strange," I said. "Whenever I'm out West, that's the feeling I get. A bunch of optimists."

"It's changed recently. A lot of people have lost money. But there was a time when folks thought that prices would continue to go up indefinitely." He sighed heavily. "My old daddy was right. He used to say, 'A tree doesn't grow to heaven.' "

We reached the gateposts of Camelback Inn and turned into the driveway. Ed dropped me off at the parking lot. He'd be in touch with me later, he said. I looked around for my car and didn't see it. Then I remembered that it wasn't my car I was looking for but Brian's. Which made me realize how much I needed sleep.

Ten minutes later I was back at the motel.

Tom was spread-eagled on my bed, snoring lightly.

Brian was sitting in one chair with his feet propped up on another. He was reading the Mutual Claims financial statement.

"Anything happen?" I asked.

"The maid tried to get in to make up the room," he said. "I told her to come back later."

I nodded and suggested that we open the connecting door between his room and mine.

The door had to be unlocked from both sides. Brian's room had already been made up.

"I'm going to borrow your bed for a while," I told him. "But first I'm going to call the office."

I brought Mark up to date on what had happened. Then I asked to have the call transferred to Irving.

"Irv," I said, "I want you to send a letter this afternoon to every customer we have on the books. I want you to put it in the strongest language you can. I want you to say that regardless of any recommendations we may have made in the past, we definitely feel that Mutual Claims stock should be sold."

"But, Brock, we've already said that, a long time ago."

"I want to say it again."

"You've found out something?"

"Not yet."

"Then what reasons shall I give?"

"Make some up."

125

"We could be sued, Brock."

"I wouldn't mind that a bit. And I want the letters to go special delivery." I started to hang up but had another thought. "I'd also like you to do a bit of detective work. I'd like a list of the telephone calls Ray Petacque made from his hotel room in New York last weekend." I gave him the name of the hotel and told him to use whatever means he thought necessary to get the information.

After that I did hang up.

I stretched out on the bed. And fell asleep at once.

– 26 –

I was in a large house. I was looking for Steve Schroeder. I knew he was there but I couldn't find him. I was walking along a hallway. Someone grabbed me. I struggled, but the person who'd grabbed me had a firm grip on my shoulder and I couldn't get away.

I opened my eyes.

Brian was shaking me.

"What time is it?" I asked thickly.

"A quarter to three," Brian said in a low voice. "Mr. Petacque's father is here."

I sat up. "Where?"

"At the door."

I jumped out of bed and hurried to the doorway that connected Brian's room with mine. I peered around the corner. The door to the outside corridor was open as far as the safety chain would permit. I looked at Tom. He was still asleep. For a moment I didn't know what to do. Then I quietly closed the connecting door, straightened my tie, ran my hand through my hair and went outside from Brian's room.

General Petacque saw me. He seemed confused. "They told me you were in there," he said.

"Well, I'm not. I'm in here."

"I want to talk to you." He came toward me slowly, leaning on his cane.

I escorted him into Brian's room. He looked around. "Where's my son?"

I turned up my palms.

"The police said he was with you."

I shrugged. I wondered whether I had the right to keep the two of them apart. Tom hadn't asked me to; he hadn't even mentioned his father. Yet something told me that he'd be better off without that additional stress, so I braced myself for a difficult confrontation.

But the confrontation didn't develop. The general limped over to a chair and eased himself into it. He seemed to be in pain. More than one kind of pain. "No doubt you feel you're doing the proper thing," he said.

I never would have believed that General Armand Petacque could have aroused such pity in me. "You'll see him eventually," I said. "He's been through a tough ordeal and he's not himself."

He glanced at the door that separated the two bedrooms. I sensed that he suspected that Brian was connected with me and that Tom was on the other side of the door. I said nothing, however, and he made no attempt to get out of the chair. "Thomas was never very good at ordeals," he said.

The pity vanished. "Has it ever occurred to you," I said, "that perhaps you're not being fair to him? That whatever his problems he's always managed to rise above them? Hell, General, he's the best securities salesman in the whole damn industry."

"I've never believed that being a good securities salesman is proof of any particular strength of character. But yes, I'm aware that Thomas has never entirely succumbed." He shifted his position in the chair and winced. "Arthritis. I dislike being old.

127

Thomas was closer to his mother when she was alive than he was to me."

And to Ed Avery, I thought. But you were the one he wanted to please. "You could clear up something for me," I said. "I'd like an honest answer to a simple question."

"I'm not known as a liar, Mr. Potter."

"Did you follow me here from Ed Avery's yesterday morning?"

"Yes."

"And tell Steve Schroeder where I was?"

"Yes."

"Why?"

"I thought you might know where Thomas was. You wouldn't tell me, but I thought you might tell Steven."

"Do you know he had me followed yesterday afternoon?"

"No," the general said after a silence. "I wasn't aware of that."

"Both of you were awfully anxious, it seems."

He glanced again at the closed door. "I buried one son this morning," he said presently. "I need the other." And for a moment I thought he was going to break down. Lines appeared in his face that hadn't been there before. His lips parted. He made a couple of sounds that were like the gasps of an asthmatic. But he tightened his grip on the cane and in so doing seemed to tighten his grip on himself. "I want him to clear his brother's reputation."

I began to understand. Schroeder had succeeded in planting the same doubts in the old man's mind about Ray's honesty that he'd tried to plant in mine. "I hardly think," I said, "that there's any need. Ray wasn't guilty of anything except not keeping up with what was going on in the business."

The general's face cleared briefly, then darkened again. "I wish I were convinced of that, Mr. Potter, but I know my children. Thomas always was the fearful one, and Raymond was the one who couldn't tell the truth. Raymond should have done better as an Army officer than he did. He could have. But there was an essential weakness in him. I recognized it. So did others. It kept

128

him from going as far as he might. The only one I've been able to have complete confidence in is my daughter."

So Tom wasn't the only one who'd had trouble with the old man. Ray'd had his share too. "I repeat," I said, "I don't think Ray was guilty of anything more than not keeping up with what was going on at Mutual Claims."

"It wasn't what was going on at Mutual Claims. It was the hotels."

"Hotels?"

"The bribes."

"What bribes?"

The general reflected. He decided that he'd gone far enough. I could see the decision in his eyes. "I won't press you to let me see my son now, but I do ask that you have him get in touch with me as soon as he's able. I feel it's extremely important. Tell him I'm at the Arizona Biltmore." He struggled to his feet.

It flashed through my mind that I might easily have run into him in the lobby the day before. But that thought was immediately eclipsed by another. "What bribes?"

"This is a family matter, Mr. Potter."

"The hell it is, General. It's a Price, Potter and Petacque matter. Tom is going to tell me, so you might as well."

He drew himself up as straight as he could. "I prefer to think that my son, whatever his weaknesses, is still strong enough to solve his problems without having to rely on you."

"Goddamn it, General, Tom is going to have his hands full with the sheriff's detectives. He saw the men who killed Ray. I'm the one who's going to have to check out anything to do with Mutual Claims. I'd be the one anyway. That's my end of the business."

The general started toward the outside door. I stepped in front of him.

"Please move," he said. "And tell my son that I expect to see him sometime today."

"No," I said.

129

The general whacked me on the ankle bone with his cane. Hard.

"Ouch!" I cried, and knelt to rub the spot he'd hit.

He walked around me and left the room.

– 27 –

I opened the connecting door and limped into my own bedroom. The ankle really hurt.

"Are you all right?" Brian asked anxiously.

"No. The son of a bitch hit me with his cane." I made my way to a chair and dropped into it. I rolled down my sock. A lump was forming.

"Want me to get some ice?"

"No. It'll be O.K. in a few minutes." I rolled up the sock and glanced at Tom. He was still sleeping. I felt deeper compassion for him than I'd ever felt before. And for Ray too.

"I eavesdropped," Brian confessed.

"Could you hear?"

"Not everything. But most of it."

"He's a miserable old bastard, but he *is* old. And I believe he *is* honest."

"He said something about hotels."

"I know. I don't know what he was talking about."

"I think I do." He took the Mutual Claims annual report from the desk and handed it to me. "Here."

I'd read the report a number of times. It was a beautiful document, with an expertly written description of the company's activities during the preceding year, colored photographs of some of the more well-known hospitals it served and of people hard at work in the Mutual Claims office, and easy-to-understand graphs. The graphs indicated steadily rising sales and profits, and the projections were optimistic. "I know what it says," I told Brian.

"Look at the financial statement."

I looked.

"It goes back to the feeling I've had right along," Brian explained. "What they do with their profits. Mutual Claims isn't like a utility of a manufacturing company. It isn't like, say"—he made a face—"Kenwood Oil. It doesn't have to keep putting the profits back into new oil wells or new plants. Some it pays out as dividends, but the rest . . . Follow me?"

In a way I did. Mutual Claims had a limited investment in plant and equipment and a low overhead. That was what made it so profitable. "Investment income," I said.

"That's in the profit and loss statement, and that's part of the picture. The other part is in the balance sheet. Where it says 'Investments.' It doesn't specify what they are. But it values them at twenty-eight million dollars."

"You think some of that may be in hotels?"

"I didn't before. I didn't know what it was in. But some of it could be hotels."

"Possibly. General Petacque also said something about bribes."

"No," Tom said very distinctly.

I gave him a startled look. He was still asleep. He was evidently dreaming.

"No, no, no," he said. Then he turned over and became quiet again.

"The company's principal investment," I said, "is the Mutual Claims Building." There was a picture of it on the cover of the report. "It's an expensive piece of property."

"I know. I was there. But it's not worth twenty-eight million dollars."

"True. Not even half of that. Let me tell you what Tom told me last night." I gave him a detailed account of Ray Petacque's visit to Tom's apartment and Tom's experiences in Phoenix.

He listened carefully. He seemed to go on listening even after I'd finished. "You don't think Mutual Claims has been deliberately overcharging the hospitals?" he asked finally.

131

"Perhaps a little," I said. "But not to the extent that would make anyone want to kill Lee Kelly." I paused. "Most hospitals aren't particularly efficient in the business area, Brian. They weren't set up as businesses. They were set up to treat sick people. The emphasis is on that. Furthermore, the big powers in a hospital are the doctors. Committees of doctors make most of the important decisions concerning the hospital—and doctors aren't notoriously good businessmen. So there's a great deal of waste in the average hospital. And to make matters even worse, federal, state, local and private money has been so forthcoming in the past decade or two that hospitals haven't really had to be efficient. That's changing now. Money is tighter. The handouts aren't as available as they used to be. But even so, what with Medicare and Medicaid and all of the group health insurance plans, and with companies like Mutual Claims to help them collect, hospitals still don't have it as tough as many businesses do."

"You're saying that they're careless."

"In many areas. You don't hear of them laying off thousands of employees in the medical field or lowering their prices, like, for instance, the automobile industry or other industries have had to do from time to time. But I'm saying, with all that, they still aren't so inefficient that they don't know how many outpatients they treat or what they treat them for or how much they have tied up in accounts receivable. One hospital may be that screwed up, but not all of them. Mutual Claims couldn't overcharge to any significant degree and get away with it. Not unless there was collusion with the various hospitals. And there again, I can imagine collusion with a few but not with all of them. Lee Kelly was killed because he'd stumbled onto something big. He didn't know it. He probably died thinking he'd uncovered nothing more than someone's incompetence. But I don't believe that it was incompetence, and while I didn't have a chance to talk it over with Tom, I don't believe that he does either. I don't even think that Ray, for all his lack of expertise, believed that it was."

Brian's eyes had narrowed. He seemed to be hanging on to every word. "Then . . . what?"

I took a deep breath. "I believe that Mutual Claims is keeping two sets of books." I picked up the annual report and threw it onto the desk. "I believe that that report is phony, that all the reports have probably been phony, that at the time we underwrote the stock we were doing so on the basis of false figures, that the whole thing is a Ponzi-like operation, and that the phoniness at the heart of the company has been covered up by what phoniness is often covered up by: growth."

"You mean like Equity Funding."

"You can find all the examples you want. The fact remains, Price, Potter and Petacque may be guilty of misrepresentation, and me in particular. Because I was the one who was supposed to check everything out."

"Oh, my God!"

"I was suckered. The fact that our customers made money on the stock doesn't change anything. I was taken in. And if there's an investigation into Mutual Claims, it will most certainly extend to Price, Potter and Petacque. What the hell, Tom and Mark are still stockholders in Mutual Claims. It'll look like we were pushing Mutual Claims for our own private gain. Or if not that, at least like we were awful fools—which we were. I think that Schroeder has been trying to tell me that. He wanted to lay it on Tom, but when he couldn't find Tom he hoped to lay it on me. To warn me that if anything came out that was damaging to him, it would also be damaging to us."

"Jesus, Brock, what are you going to do?"

"Exactly what I'd do anyway: expose whatever is wrong with Mutual Claims. It's the only way I can clear myself and our company. It won't make up for all the mistakes we've made; nothing will. But it'll help. At least nobody'll be able to say we didn't try, that when we smelled something wrong we didn't do anything."

"But how?"

"That's the problem. Eventually I'll have to take the matter to either the state's attorney here in Phoenix, or even to the Department of Justice in Washington. I'll also have to take it to the Securities and Exchange Commission. But I can't take it anywhere until I have some evidence. They have, any of those agencies, all kinds of nuts coming to them constantly with allegations of one sort or another. Even me . . . unless I have something concrete to show them, they won't pursue the thing beyond a cursory examination. And it's going to take more than that."

"What can I do to help?"

"I don't know yet. I haven't figured it all out. One thing we could do is check with all the hospitals Mutual Claims does business with. All four hundred. And come up with our own set of figures. But we don't have the staff for that, and who's to say that the hospitals would give us their figures anyway? It's a hell of a problem. Ordinarily fraud is discovered by the accountants, and in a way this one was. By Lee Kelly. But he's dead, and I don't know who else to turn to. I'm sure there are plenty of honest people at Jackley, Smith, but most of them are probably doing just what they're told. They don't have the kind of minds Kelly had. And when there's deliberate collusion between the accounting firm and its client, fraud is a bitch of a thing to prove. They can all point to the computers and say that computers don't lie. Furthermore, they undoubtedly have everything worked out to a T, so that they can back up their figures."

"Suppose you're wrong."

"I'd love to be wrong. There's nothing sadder in the world to me than finding corruption in a company that everyone believes in. But at this moment, Brian, I'd have to say that Mutual Claims may not be earning half what it says it is, it may not be worth half what it says it is. And there are probably only a handful of people at either Mutual Claims or Jackley, Smith who know the actual figures. All I can do at this point is put pressure on. I've already started. When our customers get the letter that Irving is sending

134

out today, Schroeder's going to have a lot of explaining to do. And I think I'm going to have a talk with Frank Jackley. Just to let him know that he's not excluded. Goddamn it, my ankle still hurts."

"Let me get some ice."

"Forget it. See if you can find Frank Jackley's address in the telephone directory."

Brian looked. Frank Jackley was listed. Brian wrote down the address and gave it to me.

I was putting the slip of paper into my pocket when there was a knock at the door. I tensed. "See who it is," I said to Brian. "Keep the door on the safety chain."

There was no need for the safety chain, however. Our visitors were Detectives Harlow and Eames. They wanted to take Tom back to the Mesa substation for further questioning.

− 28 −

El Camino Chiquita. The name of the street didn't mean anything to me. It didn't mean anything to the desk clerk at the motel either. She asked the cashier, who said he'd never heard of El Camino Chiquita and suggested that I ask the lady at the cigar counter. The lady at the cigar counter offered to sell me a detailed map of the city, of which she just happened to have a supply. A dollar twenty-five, please.

El Camino Chiquita: P-11. I found P. I found 11. I found the street. It was represented by a wavy line at the southern end of the Arizona Biltmore Golf Course. I was surprised, although perhaps I shouldn't have been: Frank Jackley was a neighbor of Steve Schroeder's. Schroeder's house, I recalled, adjoined the same golf course. The area was called Biltmore Estates, and mere millionaires couldn't afford to live there.

It was a quarter to six when I turned off Twenty-fourth Street onto the private drive that led to the hotel. From the top of the hill on the left the huge Wrigley mansion cast shadows over the landscaped terraces below it. I caught up with two teen-age girls in shorts who were bicycling along the drive with tennis rackets in baskets on the handlebars and followed them onto the even more private drive where the houses were.

I didn't know the address of Schroeder's house, but I recognized the place when I came to it. I braked the car and sat there for a moment, thinking. Schroeder had invited me to the house for dinner a couple of years before. He'd recently bought it, furniture and all, from the widow of a magazine publisher and was very proud of the acquisition. There were sixteen rooms, and the master bath had a sunken tub. But the cook had quit that day, and one of the maids had prepared the meal, and the food was awful. I'd come away feeling depressed—not by the meal but by the thought of a bachelor like Schroeder rattling around by himself in such a large place.

From the outside the house appeared unchanged. No additions, no subtractions, nothing to indicate that the place had ever changed hands. I wondered whether Schroeder still liked it. Whether he'd ever liked it, really. And whether he'd found a girlfriend to share it with him. During the time I'd known him I'd never heard any mention of a woman in his life. He was strictly a loner. The cheese broker's son from Green Bay, Wisconsin, was living out his dreams. But what limited dreams they were.

Dreams are dreams, though, and when your dream is threatened, what do you do? Do you kill?

I had a sudden hollow feeling at the pit of my stomach.

I drove on.

Jackley's house was smaller. But the car in the driveway was a Rolls. A silver one, at that.

I parked my car behind it, got out, skirted a couple of orange trees that seemed about to topple under the weight of all the oranges that were growing on them, and pushed the button beside the front door.

136

The door was opened by a teen-age boy in white tennis shorts and a T-shirt. He'd evidently been expecting someone else, for the look he gave me was a startled one.

"Is Mr. Jackley home?" I asked.

He called over his shoulder, "Pa, it's for you." He received no answer and called again, more loudly.

"Don't holler," came a voice from another room. "I'm not deaf." And a moment later Frank Jackley appeared, a tall, saturnine man who seemed to have more bones than flesh. His face did a number of things when he saw me, but he finally managed to smile. "Well, I'll be darned."

"I just happened to be in the neighborhood," I said, "and I thought I'd drop in."

He called over his shoulder, much as his son had, "Maggie, we have company."

His wife joined us. She was as short as he was tall, a compact little woman with a beautiful suntan. I couldn't recall ever having met her, and she apparently couldn't recall ever having met me either, for she gave me a quick little smile and turned inquiring eyes on her husband.

"Brockton Peters," he said. "You've heard me speak of him."

"Of course," she said automatically.

We shook hands. She had a firm grip. She too was in a tennis outfit.

Their son looked beyond me. "Here they come now," he said.

I turned. The two girls I'd seen on bicycles were pedaling up the driveway.

The girls names were Diane-something and Melody-something-else. In the confusion of the moment I couldn't tell which was which. Jackley's wife explained that she and the kids were going to play a few games of tennis and then they were all going to have a sort of pick-up supper, for which she hoped I'd stay. I said that I'd like to but couldn't. No one seemed to know quite what to do with me at that point, and we all just stood there in

137

the entrance hall until I told Jackley that I'd be glad to have a drink with him instead of the pick-up supper.

"Of course, of course," he said, and led me through the living room to a large glassed-in family room that offered a view of an obviously new tennis court and the golf course beyond.

While he was fussing over the ice and the bottles, I saw his wife and son and the two girls emerge from the other side of the house and position themselves on the court. Jackley told me twice what a pleasant surprise it was to see me, but the expression on his face didn't match the words. A surprise I might be, but a pleasant surprise I plainly wasn't.

"Out here for the funeral, I suppose," he said.

"Among other things," I said.

He'd started to give me my drink. He pulled his hand back as if he'd changed his mind, then realized what he was doing and held the glass out again. He said, "Business, no doubt."

I nodded.

He settled himself in a white leather lounge chair and extended his long legs. "Terrible thing," he said. "Such fine people. Why is it the good ones always have to be the ones to go? And in this case in such a miserable, senseless way. It makes a person wonder what it's all about."

My attention was diverted by the scene outside. The tennis players had just started to volley when two apricot-colored poodles darted out from behind a hedge and onto the court. They began to chase the ball. Mrs. Jackley proceeded to chase them. In so doing she missed a shot, and the ball rolled up against the fence. One of the poodles got it. Mrs. Jackley grabbed the poodle and took the ball away from it, whereupon the other dog sat up and begged. Mrs. Jackley left the court with a dog under each arm and came toward the house. Presently a door slammed.

"And stay there," Mrs. Jackley said in a loud voice.

The door slammed again.

Moments later the two poodles were in the family room, sniffing at my shoes.

The volleying resumed, and so did my conversation with Jackley. "Yes, terrible," I said.

"I didn't see Tom at the funeral this morning," Jackley said cautiously.

"He's been under the weather."

"Nothing serious, I hope."

"Nothing that clearing up the murders won't cure, in my opinion." I paused. "Have the sheriff's men questioned you?"

"No." He kept his eyes on me. There was no trust at all in them. "I don't imagine they will. There's really nothing I can contribute."

"Unless, of course, there's a connection between Ray and Blanche's murders and the murder of Lee Kelly."

He didn't ask me how I knew about Kelly. He simply said, "Do you think there might be?" But his voice had dropped so low that I could barely hear him.

I picked up one of the dogs and scratched him behind the ears. He licked my hand. The other dog went into his begging act. "Who am I to say?" I replied. I put the dog down and he ran over to Jackley. Jackley brushed him aside with his foot. He trotted into the living room. The begger followed him. "Nice dogs," I told Jackley.

He seemed not to have heard me.

"From little hints and rumors I've been picking up," I went on, "I've become a bit worried about Mutual Claims. Any other company, I might not give it a second thought. But Mutual Claims, well, I feel a special sense of responsibility. You can understand that, I imagine."

He didn't say whether he could or couldn't.

"What I'm trying to say, Frank, is I've always kind of taken your figures for granted. I've done a certain amount of checking—talked to people at some of the hospitals and at Mutual Claims. But what could they tell me? All they could say—the people at the hospitals—is yes, they signed a contract with Mutual Claims and everything is working out fine. And the people at Mutual

139

Claims—all they could tell me is yes, they've got so-and-so many hospitals signed up and they're about to sign up so-and-so many more. But I'm beginning to wonder whether there isn't more to it than that, whether there's something I should have been looking into but wasn't. I'd feel bad if that were true. Like I was negligent." I sipped some Scotch.

Jackley said nothing.

I waited.

Still he said nothing.

I took another sip of my drink.

"Why don't you go ahead and say it?" Jackley said finally.

"Say what?"

"Whatever it is that's on your mind. You seem to be insinuating something. Why don't you just come out with it?"

"I'm not insinuating anything, Frank. I'm worried, that's all. Because if something were wrong at Mutual Claims, it would make me look bad. And you too. After all, your company's the only one who's ever audited their books. If it turned out that things aren't what they're supposed to be, you'd be in kind of a sticky situation."

"I'm not sure that I like this conversation, Brock. I always felt that we were friends. And I'd hate to have to be tactless enough to remind you that you're a guest in my house at the moment."

"Of course. And your Scotch is very good. But it's because we are friends, don't you see, or at least because we've known each other for quite a while, that I feel I should mention it. I can't very well talk to Steve. And I hope that you won't either. I'd like this to remain strictly between ourselves. But I *am* worried."

"I don't know what you expect me to say. I think you're moving into rather dangerous ground, though."

"I hope not. I hope that I'll find that everything is just fine." I took a final sip of the drink and stood up. "I have to be going. Perhaps I'll drop around and see you at the office in a day or two. Meanwhile I'd appreciate it if you'd keep what I said confidential."

140

Jackley got up too. "Naturally."

He walked me to the front door. We shook hands. I told him he had a beautiful house. He thanked me and closed the door.

Instead of going to the car, I walked around the side of the house and out to the tennis court. I waited until one of the young girls scored a point, then interrupted the game to tell Mrs. Jackley goodbye.

"Sure you won't stay for supper?" she said.

"Positive," I assured her. "But thanks anyway."

She returned to the game. I managed to get close enough to the windows of the family room to see what was going on inside.

Jackley was talking on the telephone.

– 29 –

"Mr. Price called," Brian said. "Right after you left. Wants you to call him back at home. What did Jackley have to say?"

"Jackley has a new tennis court," I said. "Tennis courts aren't cheap these days. A good one costs ten, twelve thousand. And this was a good one."

"So?"

"He also has a nice house in front of it. About a quarter of a million, I'd say. And a very pretty Rolls-Royce. And a couple of poodles that look as if they get groomed at Elizabeth Arden. Jackley's leading the good life."

"But what did he say?"

"Nothing."

The corners of Brian's mouth turned downward.

"Not really nothing," I amended. "He reminded me that I was a guest in his house. He's not what you'd call a talkative man. Never was. But before I'd even pulled my car out of the driveway he was on the phone, and you can guess who was at the other end."

141

Brian nodded. "So what do we do now?"

"Nothing. For the moment, at least. Wait till people get the letter Irving is sending out. Any word from Tom?"

Brian shook his head. "I'd kind of like to find out about those hotels."

"So would I. In fact, all the investments Mutual Claims has. But let's wait. Tomorrow's another day." I went to the telephone and dialed.

Mark must have been sitting with the telephone on his lap. He answered before the first ring was completed.

"I thought I'd better tell you," he said. "Daisy's on her way to Phoenix."

"No!"

"Is that going to complicate things for you?"

"It probably won't make any difference. But what happened?"

"I called her after I talked to you. I said that you'd found Tom and he's all right. I stressed that there was nothing to worry about. I even said that he'd probably be home in a couple of days. She seemed very relieved. I offered to come out to Great Neck and take her to dinner, and she said fine, she'd like that. So when I left the office I drove out there, and when I got there her sister said she'd left for Phoenix. The boy's still with her sister, but Daisy's—well, she's probably there by now."

"What time did she leave?"

"I think about three o'clock, our time."

I glanced at my watch. Twenty minutes to eight, Mountain Time. Twenty minutes to ten in New York. "She's just about landing, I imagine. Do you know where she was planning to stay?"

"She didn't tell her sister. I don't think she was sure."

I began to feel uneasy. "What made her change her mind? Did her sister tell you that?"

"She got a phone call from this friend of Tom's. I think the name is Avery. Do you know him?"

"Yes."

"Well, he said Tom needed her, Tom wanted her to come out."

The uneasiness mounted. "Stay by the telephone," I said. "I'll call you back." I hung up.

I dialed Ed's number.

No answer.

I dialed again, in case I'd made a mistake.

No answer.

"Anything wrong?" Brian asked. "You look nervous."

"Get on the other telephone," I said. "Call the airport. I want to know what time they have flights coming in from New York. All airlines."

Brian went into the other bedroom and picked up the telephone.

I called Mark again. "I just tried Avery's number," I said. "He's not home. He may be at the airport, meeting Daisy. I can't imagine why he sent for her. I don't understand it."

"You sound upset."

"I am, a little. But I'm glad you told me."

"Is Tom with you?"

"He was. They took him back to the station this afternoon for more questioning."

"How is he?"

"Worn out. But he had a few hours' sleep. I think he's going to be O.K., Mark. We're up to our ears in trouble, though."

"I figured we might be. I saw a copy of a letter Irving sent out this afternoon. I had a fit. He said you told him to write it, though."

"I did." I told him what I suspected, what I was trying to do. "There's one other problem," I added. "The stock that you and Tom own."

"I've been wrestling with my conscience all afternoon. If we sell it, they could claim we were taking advantage of inside information. If we keep it, we're liable to take an awful beating. So far I haven't done anything."

"It may be necessary to take the loss, Mark. O.K.?"

"I'm inclined to agree with you."

"Good boy." I saw Brian through the open doorway. He'd put down the telephone and was coming back into my room. "You can do one more thing, though, Mark. Call Daisy's sister. Ask her who besides us knew that Daisy was in Great Neck. Daisy may have told somebody."

"You're worried about her, aren't you?"

"I don't know why I should be. It's probably perfectly all right. But yes, I am."

"I'll see what I can find out. Will you be in your room for a while?"

"Most likely. If not, tell Brian."

We hung up.

Brian handed me a list of flight numbers and times. "These are the through flights from New York," he said. "But there's an awful lot of other ways to get here for somebody who can't get on one of the through flights. Like Mr. Petacque—he changed in Chicago. You can also make connections in St. Louis, Detroit, Kansas City, Dallas, Washington, any number of places. Why are you shaking your head?"

"It's hopeless. Mrs. Petacque left New York this afternoon for Phoenix. She probably did get on one of the through flights. She's probably here already. I had in mind to go to the airport and wait around, hoping to run into her. But now I'm afraid it's too late."

"Most likely."

"Ed Avery's the one who called her and told her to come. He probably knows what flight she's on, but he's not home."

"I wonder why he did that."

"So do I."

We fell silent.

I waited for Mark to call back.

144

The telephone didn't ring.

But someone knocked at the door.

"Who is it?" I called.

"It's Tom."

I let him in. He was alone. He had a sheet of paper in his hand. "This is the best I could do," he said wearily, holding out the sheet of paper.

It took it. It was a facsimile of an artist's sketch. A man's face. Apparently Mexican. "Who is it?" I asked.

"The guy who killed Ray and Blanche."

Brian looked at the picture over my shoulder.

"What's his name?" I asked.

"Nobody knows," Tom replied.

– 30 –

I took Brian aside. "Is it . . . ?"

"I don't think so. But they could be friends."

I went back to Tom. He'd seated himself on the bed. He'd clasped his hands between his knees and was gazing forlornly at the carpet. The hours at the Mesa substation hadn't done him any good. He was slipping back into depression. And that we didn't need. "What happened?" I asked sharply. "What did they want?"

He shook his head sadly. "They wanted me to tell them everything again. Then they brought in this artist. They made me work with him. I did the best I could. I'm sorry."

"How accurate is this picture?"

"Pretty accurate, I think. I did the best I could. I've caused everybody a lot of trouble. I should have gone to the police right away. It was a mistake. I'm sorry." He sighed deeply. "I'm awfully tired. Do you have any more pills?"

"No. The pills belonged to Ed—remember? And if you're tired you don't need any pills; you'll sleep anyway. But what you need is a good drink and a good meal. You haven't eaten all day."

"I'm not hungry."

It was a question of priorities. There was Daisy. There was Ed. There was the call from Mark. But first and foremost there was Tom. I couldn't let him slide downhill any farther. "I'll tell you what we're going to do. I'm expecting a call from Mark. Brian will wait here for it. You and I are going out for something to eat."

"I'm not hungry."

"Well, you can keep me company." I turned to Brian. "You wait here. Order something from room service. And have them put another bed in my room. There's a Trader Vic's a few blocks from here. Tom and I are going over there. You can get in touch with me there if it's important."

Brian nodded.

"I don't want to eat," Tom said. "I'm not hungry."

I pulled him to his feet. He insisted that he didn't want to go out, that he was tired, that he was sorry to be causing everyone so much trouble, that he hadn't shaved, that he didn't know where his toothbrush was, that I kept making him do things he didn't want to do. But I got him to the door. And down the steps. And into the car. And over to the restaurant.

He did need a shave. He did look as if he'd slept in his clothes. He did walk like someone who was recovering from a three-day drinking spree. But after a few minutes in the restaurant he began to get hold of himself, as I'd hoped he would. For if there was any one place other than his office and his home where he felt comfortable and authoritative, it was in a restaurant. During most of his working life he'd had to entertain, and he was good at it, and he knew he was good at it.

It wasn't that he drank much that evening. Or ate more than a few bites of the Cantonese duck that he ordered. Or suddenly became vigorous. But he did seem to be coming to terms with himself. Even in the dim light of the would-be Polynesian room I could see his eyes brighten.

I avoided topics that would cause him anxiety. I said nothing about Daisy's departure for Phoenix, nothing about the funeral. I didn't even tell him that his father had come looking for him. On the other hand, I didn't pretend that either of us was in Arizona on a pleasure trip. I told him about my visit to Jackley's house and about the letter I'd instructed Irving to send out. He seemed to understand that I was trying to get us off the hook and at the same time to put pressure on Schroeder, and he approved. I even brought up the subject of the loss that he was liable to take in Mutual Claims stock.

"So be it," he said. "I should have sold the damn stuff when you told me to."

"It's going to cost Mark a bundle too," I said, "but he's willing. And in the long run, maybe the stock will come back."

"Is your thinking the same as mine?" he asked. "That the figures Schroeder's been reporting are inflated?"

That was the most with-it question he'd asked, and I felt further encouraged. "That's my suspicion," I said. "I think he's been reporting inflated profits from the hospital end of the business to cover up losses in investments."

"The bastard."

I changed the subject. "The picture that you showed me—the sheriff's office has no idea who the man is?"

"Not yet."

"But you said there were two men."

"That's true. And I don't know which did the actual shooting. It may have been one, it may have been the other, it may have been both. But I only got a good look at one of them—the one who turned around and fired the gun at me. God, Brock, it was awful. He dropped Ray—I could almost hear his head hit the floor. I— do we have to talk about it?"

"Not talking about it isn't going to make you feel any better, Tom."

"No, I suppose not. All right. You know how the house is built? There's this door that leads from the house into the garage. I saw the door open. I saw a man coming into the garage. He had his hands under Ray's armpits. They were carrying him headfirst. Then I saw the other man, who was carrying his feet, but at that moment apparently the first one realized there were headlights shining into the garage. He dropped Ray, whipped this gun out and aimed it at me. He's the one I got a good look at. He's the one I showed you the picture of. God, I wish I were home. I'm going to call Daisy when we get back to the motel. But don't worry—I'm not going to leave Phoenix until we get this thing cleared up. I hope you'll let me help."

"Daisy's fine. Mark talked to her this afternoon. She was at her sister's. You are helping. You've helped a lot."

"They think the man is a Mexican. That's what I said he looked like, and that's what the picture shows. They said Phoenix is full of Mexicans. Many of them are here as illegal aliens. They come across the border all the time, into Texas, Arizona, California—you can practically walk across the river at certain times. It's a terrible problem, Eames said. They don't even know how many illegal aliens there are in the U.S. anymore. Maybe five million, maybe ten million. They keep catching them and sending them back to where they came from, but then they come back again. The system's completely broken down, Eames said. And most of the illegal aliens are Mexican. They need work permits in order to get jobs, but there's a business in fake work permits like you wouldn't believe. They cost about two hundred and fifty dollars here, but in Mexico you can get them for about seventy. And there are people who make a business of smuggling Mexicans into the country. So much a head. They bring them in in trucks and every which way. The trouble is, according to Harlow, that people here give them jobs without work permits, because the wetbacks work for less than the minimum wage. If they could just stop that, stop people hiring them, they'd have a big part of the problem licked.

"Anyway, they're going to have a hard time identifying this guy unless he has some kind of a record. Just a picture isn't enough. They don't have pictures of all the wetbacks. Anyone who has a record, though, anyone like that—there's a chance. The records, many of them, have photographs. And fingerprints. Anyone who's been deported once, or who's been involved in a crime, has a record.

"They can't ask the FBI for help unless they have a name or fingerprints. The FBI has records of names and fingerprints, but just a picture isn't enough. And that's all they have right now—that's all I was able to give them."

"They didn't get any fingerprints from the house or from the car?"

"They didn't say. And I can't remember whether the guy was wearing gloves or not. I tried to, but I can't. However, they were going to take the picture over to the Immigration and Naturalization people. Depending on how accurate the picture is, they may get some help there. The immigration people, they deal with illegal immigrants all the time. Their investigators are trained to remember faces. It's amazing, Harlow said, how good some of them are at it. But if this guy has no record, or if nobody happens to remember him, then it's a different story—then there isn't much hope. Christ, I'm tired, Brock. I wonder if another drink would help."

"It won't do any harm."

He summoned a waiter. "Another Mai Tai."

The waiter departed.

Tom stared at the tablecloth. "I was wrong to hide out over there at that retreat for two days. I can see that now. I should have gone right to the police. But I was—well, it's a terrible thing, Brock, getting the way I get. All those years—you'd think somewhere along the line I'd have got over it."

"It's more like a susceptibility, I think. But most of the time

149

you're fine, Tom. In fact, you're so good that most people in the business would give their eyeteeth to be like you."

"I'm always afraid, though. Afraid that it might come back. And it has. I feel shitty right now."

"You're not talking shitty. You're talking sense."

"But I feel shitty. I feel like I let everybody down. I should have gone to the police right away. Maybe they'd have caught those guys by now. As it is, they could be a thousand miles away."

"I'm not so concerned about them. I'm concerned about who hired them, and why."

"I'm concerned about them too, Brock. They killed my brother and my sister-in-law."

The waiter appeared with the drink.

And I saw Brian standing near the entrance to the room. "Excuse me," I said, and got up quickly. I hurried over to where he was standing. "What's up?"

He looked terribly worried. "Mark called. He had trouble reaching Daisy's sister. She was out. She doesn't know whether Daisy told anyone else where she was going or not. But she did say that Daisy talked to Tom's father. He called, to find out if she was there, and she thought she'd better talk to him. So he knew."

"And God knows who he told."

"Right. But that's not what's bothering me, that's not why I came over. This friend of yours, this Ed Avery, he came over a few minutes ago. He wanted to know how Tom was, he said. I didn't know whether I ought to be the one to ask him about Mrs. Petacque or not, but I did. And, Brock, he says he never called her, he never told her Tom wanted her to come to Phoenix."

150

I managed to get through the rest of the meal without showing alarm. And to drive Tom back to the motel. And to talk him out of calling Daisy. It was almost midnight in New York, I argued; he'd disturb the entire household.

He went to bed and was soon asleep. I told Brian to keep an eye on him until I got back. Then I got into the car and drove to Ed's.

Ed was almost as upset as I was. "What's this about my calling Daisy and telling her to come to Phoenix?" he demanded.

"That's what I want to know," I said. "Her sister says you did."

"I didn't."

"Then someone must have used your name."

"It's what I was afraid of: someone using her to get at Tom." He lit one of those cigarillos of his and began to pace the floor. "Her sister's house was no place for her to go. She should have gone someplace no one would have thought of. Damn. Damn, damn, *damn*."

"Wouldn't she have recognized your voice?"

"I doubt it. I haven't seen her since that night at the house-warming party. I've seen Tom, of course, and talked to him on the telephone, but Daisy—no, I don't think so."

"Where were you around eight o'clock?"

"At the Quilted Bear." He frowned. "Why?"

"I tried to call you. What's the Quilted Bear?"

"A restaurant. I sometimes eat there when I don't feel like cooking. It's about a mile from here." He paused. "Does Tom know?"

"I'm trying to keep it from him, but I don't know how long I'll be able to."

Ed spilled ashes on the floor, but didn't notice. "Daisy would have called me when she landed, I should think. She knew I was looking after Tom."

"Or me. Mark had told her I'd located him." I reflected. "But maybe not. He might not have told her where I was."

"What are you going to do?"

"Go to the police."

"Do you think that's wise? It could be she's all right."

"I'm not going to take any chances."

"If you do that, it'll get into the newspapers. Tom is sure to find out."

"Maybe not."

"Damn," he said.

I left. But instead of going to the Mesa substation I went to the Arizona Biltmore.

There was little activity in the lobby. A few people were sitting around, and a few others were playing cards, but the majority of guests had retired.

I found the house phones and asked the operator to connect me with General Petacque. She rang. A woman answered.

"Daisy?" I asked quickly.

"No," the woman said. "This is Mrs. Lang."

My heart sank. Clarissa Lang. Tom's sister. "This is Brockton Potter. I'd like to come up if I may. It's important."

I heard a voice in the background. I heard the woman say, "Brockton Potter. He wants to come up."

The woman spoke into the telephone again. "I'm sorry, Mr. Potter. My father has gone to bed, and I was just getting ready to."

"Tell your father that I'm about to have him arrested for the kidnapping of your sister-in-law."

"I beg your pardon?"

I repeated the statement.

There was a silence. She must have covered the mouthpiece of the telephone, for I couldn't hear anything.

Her father came on the line. "I have nothing further to discuss with you. . . . What's this about a kidnapping?"

"There's reason to believe that Daisy's been kidnapped and that you're involved. You can discuss it either with me or with the police. Take your choice."

There was another silence. "Perhaps you'd better come up." He gave me the number of his suite.

The door was open, and Clarissa Lang was standing there in a dressing gown. I'd never met her, but her resemblance to Tom was striking. Except that the square jaw and narrow face suited him better than they suited her. "Come in," she said.

I walked into the living room of the two-bedroom suite. General Petacque was seated on a sofa, his cane between his legs. He too was in a dressing gown.

"What's this about a kidnapping?" he asked again.

I didn't sit down. I took a position out of reach of the cane and said, "Did you speak to Daisy this afternoon?"

"Answer my question."

"*You* answer *my* question. Did you?"

"I don't know that it's any concern of yours."

"I take it you did, then. How did you know where to find her?"

The general relented. "Yes, I spoke with her. I've been trying to locate her ever since Tuesday. It never occurred to me, for some reason, that she might be staying with her sister. I called the apartment in New York repeatedly. The maid kept answering and saying that everyone was away, she didn't know where. Actually, it was Clarissa who suggested that Daisy might have gone to her sister's."

"Why did you call her?"

"Mr. Potter," Clarissa Lang said sharply, "there's no need for you to speak to my father in that tone."

I ignored her. So did the general. He said, "I thought that her place was here with me, with the rest of the family. It was her duty to be with us."

153

"Did you tell her that?"

The general hesitated. "I was going to. I felt most strongly about it. But no, I didn't. When I asked her why she was at her sister's, she said that Thomas had told her to go there. He told her that she was in danger. I didn't understand, but I—no, I didn't tell her to come here. What did Thomas mean, she was in danger?"

"Just that. And he was right. Did you tell Steve Schroeder that you'd talked to her?"

There was another silence.

"Did you?"

"He came back to the hotel with us after the funeral. He was here when I made the call."

I hadn't intended to sit down, but suddenly I did. On the first chair I could find. "You fool!"

"Mr. Potter!" his daughter said angrily.

"You miserable, arrogant, thick-skulled idiot!"

The general got red in the face. Then he began to look unsure of himself, even frightened. "What's happened?" he asked unsteadily.

"Someone called Daisy at her sister's this afternoon and claimed to be Ed Avery. He said that Tom wanted her to come to Phoenix. She left her sister's to come here—and hasn't been heard from since."

Clarissa Lang had been standing, but she too sat down. As suddenly as I had. On the sofa next to her father. "Oh, no!"

The general put his hand first to his mouth, then to his forehead. "Claimed to be Ed Avery?" he asked hoarsely.

"Yes. Except that Ed never made the call."

"He must have. That man was never trustworthy. I knew him better than most. I—"

"Steve Schroeder wants to keep Tom quiet. He wants to keep me quiet. He'll stop at nothing."

"You're mistaken. He—he's been trying to protect Raymond's reputation. Raymond—"

"Ray was innocent."

"No. No, he wasn't." He lowered his head. He uttered a couple of those asthmatic gasps. His daughter put her arm around him.

"If you're talking about the murder of Lee Kelly," I said, "Ray had nothing to do with that, except in the most indirect way."

The general raised his head. He had tears in his eyes. "You know about that?"

"Yes, but how did *you* find out?"

"Raymond told me. He came to Sarasota. I—I'm the one who advised him to talk to Thomas. I—I didn't know that Thomas would be unequal to the situation. My sons—I tried to do the right thing, to raise them properly. I—"

"Ray had nothing to do with Kelly's murder. He was feeling unnecessarily guilty."

"But there's also the hotels. He's the one who recommended that Steven buy them. He was paid off by the previous owners, who were trying to unload."

"Which hotels?"

"The one here in Phoenix, the Arroyo. And the one in Jamaica, the Royal Montego. And the one in St. Thomas, the Starfish Beach."

"Did Ray tell you that?"

"No. Steven did. He bought them at the wrong time. They were a mistake. The Arroyo is too far out. And people have stopped going to the Caribbean like they used to."

"I very much doubt that Ray had anything to do with those purchases. My guess is that Schroeder bought those hotels on his own. He's property-hungry. He's good at one thing—computer programming—but he'd like to be an expert at everything. God knows what other bad investments he's made besides those hotels, both for the business and for himself personally. He's been selling his Mutual Claims stock right along. He's probably been investing the money in real estate—badly. And in order to get the top price for his stock, he's been exaggerating the profits of the company."

The general blinked. "You don't think Raymond accepted

155

bribes?" He seemed unable to comprehend anything beyond that. Nothing that Schroeder did mattered to him.

"I doubt it. But meanwhile there's Daisy."

"But why would Steven want to do anything to her?"

"To keep Tom from exposing him. To keep me from exposing him."

"He wouldn't harm a woman."

"The hell he wouldn't."

"He wouldn't harm a woman," the general repeated.

"A cornered man will do anything," I said. "And I believe that Steve Schroeder feels cornered." I got up. "And for whatever it's worth to you, if anything happens to Daisy, you can thank yourself for having contributed. Good night, General."

I walked out, leaving him and his daughter sitting side by side on the sofa.

– 32 –

It was a long drive from the Arizona Biltmore to the building on West First Street in Mesa. On the way I tried to convince myself that my fears were groundless. Daisy might have changed her mind. She might have gone back to the apartment in New York. She might have returned to her sister's. She might be in Phoenix, safe and comfortable in a hotel.

I tried. But I didn't succeed. In fact, my fears grew more acute. Schroeder had been with the general when the general made the call. Schroeder had probably been the one who urged him to make it, to keep trying various places until he finally found her. Then Schroeder, or someone acting for him, had placed his own call, pretending to be Ed. With flight information and a promise to meet her at the airport. She might have been surprised to find Schroeder instead of Ed at the airport, but she would have gone with him; she knew him.

Camelback Road to Scottsdale Road, Scottsdale Road to Arizona State University, then turn left. But I turned too soon and found myself on a street that I didn't recognize. I went back to Scottsdale Road, swung south and continued until I reached the right street, Apache Boulevard. It took me into the business district of Mesa. There, however, I got confused between First Street and First Avenue. It was ten minutes past one before I found the little brick building that I remembered.

"SHERIFF'S OFFICE, MESA SUBSTATION, INFORMATION, COMPLAINTS, PULL."

I pulled. The door swung open. I hurried into the room where I'd spent so many hours the night before. It was as if I'd never left. Some of the same officers were on duty. They wanted to know what my problem was. I told them I had to see Harlow or Eames. I was informed that both of them were off duty.

"I have to see them," I insisted. "I have important new information about the Petacque killings."

There was no argument, no hesitation. One of the patrolmen picked up the nearest telephone and dialed. He spoke to Harlow.

"He'll be here in a few minutes," the patrolman said.

I waited. And drank some Pepsi-Cola. And smoked a couple of cigarettes.

Harlow had evidently got in touch with Eames, for the two of them arrived together. Both looked as if they'd dressed hastily and both needed a shave. They took me into one of the private offices.

"All right," Eames said briskly, "what's this about new information."

"I believe that Tom Petacque's wife has been kidnapped," I said.

Eames sat down slowly behind the desk. Harlow remained standing. Both of them stared at me.

"What?" Harlow asked.

"Tom called his wife three nights ago. He warned her that she might be in danger. He talked her into taking their son and going away. She went to stay with her sister, who lives on Long Island.

Today she got a telephone call from someone who claimed to be Ed Avery, telling her Tom wanted her to come to Phoenix. She left her sister's. No one's heard from her since. I believe that she was kidnapped, here in Phoenix."

"What danger?" Harlow asked.

"Kidnapping's a serious charge," Eames said.

"What makes you think she was?" Harlow asked.

"Is there something you haven't told us?" Eames asked.

"Yes," I said. "A lot."

Both of them looked at me. There was anger in their eyes. But neither of them spoke.

I'd lined up what I was going to say. Now I said it. "The murder of Ray and Blanche Petacque is related to another murder which took place here in Phoenix around Christmastime. A man named Lee Kelly was killed. You probably didn't handle the case, but maybe you know about it. He was a young employee with the accounting firm of Jackley, Smith. He was killed, I'm convinced, because he'd stumbled across something in the books of Mutual Claims Company which indicated fraud. He told Ray Petacque, who told Steven Schroeder. Kelly was killed to keep him quiet. But Ray Petacque kept trying to get at the truth. He told his brother. His brother came out here to help him but got here too late. Ray and his wife were killed for the same reason Kelly was, or at least Ray was—his wife was probably killed simply because she happened to be there. I'm here to look into Mutual Claims. Schroeder doesn't want me to. He intends to use Tom's wife— her safety—as a weapon to keep me from doing it."

"Are you saying that the Petacques weren't killed by those men Petacque's brother saw?" Harlow asked.

"No. They probably were. And perhaps Kelly too. What I'm saying is that they were hired by Steve Schroeder."

"Who's Steve Schroeder?" Harlow asked.

I couldn't believe that they didn't know. But evidently they didn't. "Chairman of the board and chief executive officer of Mutual Claims Company."

158

"The building on Central Avenue?" Eames asked.

"Yes."

"And you're saying that the chairman of the board of that company hired a couple of killers to shoot the Petacques?"

"I am."

"And kidnap this woman from New York?"

"Yes."

Harlow still had anger in his eyes. But Eames appeared to be just plain doubtful.

"What evidence do you have of all this?" he asked presently.

"None," I replied. "But I know I'm right. He even had me followed." I explained about the brown car and gave them the license number.

"Why didn't you tell us any of this last night?" Harlow demanded. "Why didn't Mr. Petacque? Why didn't anybody?"

"Because none of us has any proof."

"In other words, it's just a theory."

"It's more than a theory. I'm positive I'm right. But I don't have any proof."

"And the kidnapping?"

"I don't have any proof of that either. But you'd better do something about it."

"Let's talk to the lieutenant," Harlow said to Eames.

They left the office.

Although they were gone for less than ten minutes, it seemed much longer. And as I sat there in the small, sparsely furnished office, I realized that what seemed so certain to me probably sounded like wild, unfounded accusations to them. They didn't even know who Schroeder was. They couldn't imagine how much was at stake for him.

I also realized that the evidence I needed was almost impossible to get without the cooperation of someone at Mutual Claims or someone at Jackley, Smith. It was easy to evaluate a company when you had access to its true figures. But without that . . .

They returned.

159

"Give us a description of Mrs. Petacque," Harlow said.

I gave them as accurate a description as I could.

They left me alone again.

Something was happening. Even though I couldn't see into the other offices, I sensed an acceleration in the tempo of the place. Perhaps it was a change in the noise level, a quickening of footsteps—but things were being done.

An officer in uniform opened the door and looked at me, seemingly out of sheer curiosity, then left, closing the door behind him.

Messages were going out, I imagined. Perhaps to the sheriff's office downtown. Perhaps to the FBI. Or the police in New York.

I'd accomplished something. A search for Daisy was under way. But the feeling of hopelessness returned. Without evidence, without proof . . .

The two detectives returned with a third man. They introduced him as the lieutenant who was in charge of the station. He made me repeat my story.

"Why didn't you tell the detectives this last night?" he asked when I finished. His voice was flat, his face without expression.

"Because I couldn't prove anything. But now that I have told you, what are you going to do?"

"We're going to question Mr. Schroeder."

"And what do you think he's going to tell you?"

"The truth, we hope."

I sighed. "He's going to tell you that he doesn't know what you're talking about, that I'm crazy and ought to be locked up and sued for slander, and that there's nothing wrong with his company and he can prove it."

"If he can prove it . . ."

"I know, I know. That's the whole trouble. But I'm right. And Daisy's disappeared."

"That's only a supposition on your part. But we've started the ball rolling. If she arrived in Phoenix, we'll find her. And those two men Mr. Petacque saw at his brother's house—we're doing

160

all we can to find out who they are. Tomorrow morning Detective Harlow here is going to round up someone from the Immigration and Naturalization office."

"Tomorrow morning," I said dully.

"*This* morning, actually. In a few hours."

I nodded. I looked from one to the other. I didn't see what I wanted to see on the face of any of them. Suddenly I felt very weary. "Well," I said, "I've told you what I can. May I go now?"

No one said that I couldn't. The only one who spoke was the lieutenant. He said, "You'll be available, I assume."

"I'll be available," I said.

And I drove back to the motel.

Tom was asleep on my bed. A folding bed had been set up next to it. Brian was in the adjoining room.

"Have they found Mrs. Petacque?" he asked.

"No," I said. "They've just started to look."

I stretched out on the folding bed and, in spite of everything, fell asleep. With my clothes on.

– 33 –

And when I awoke a strange period began. A period in which all kinds of things could have happened, should have happened, yet didn't happen. A period of calm, almost of normalcy.

It was eight o'clock. I'd forgotten to draw the drapes across the sliding glass door that opened onto the balcony, and the sun was like a flashlight beamed directly at my face. For a few moments I was confused. I thought I was in New York and I couldn't understand what was wrong; sunlight never flooded my bedroom like that. Then I had the sensation that my feet were unusually heavy and realized that I was wearing my shoes. In fact, all my clothes. At which point I recalled where I was, and memories of the night before assaulted me.

The feeling of hopelessness returned. It amounted almost to despair.

I turned over.

Tom was sitting up in bed, scratching himself. "Hi," he said.

Should I tell him about Daisy? Sooner or later the story would be in the newspapers or on television.

I decided not to. Not for a while. "Hi," I said.

"You slept in your clothes," he observed.

"You need a shave," I observed. I got up and went to the open doorway to Brian's room. Brian was sitting in a chair in his underwear, eating an orange.

"Did you—?" he began.

I put my finger to my lips.

He nodded. "Want an orange?" And without waiting for an answer, he walked out onto his balcony, leaned over the rail and picked two oranges from the tree below. It was an effort for him to reach them, and he almost fell, but he managed to get a couple of nice ones. He gave them to me.

I tossed one to Tom and began to peel the other with my fingers. Juice squirted into my face.

Brian joined us. No one spoke. We simply worked on the oranges.

My feeling of hopelessness continued.

Tom wiped some juice from his chin. "I really do need a shave," he remarked, "but I don't know where my things are." He'd bought some toilet articles and some furnishings before going to the airport in New York, he explained, but he couldn't remember what he'd done with them.

"They're probably still at the Renewal Center," I said.

"No," said Brian. "They're in the trunk of Ed's station wagon."

"Are you sure?" Tom asked.

"I think so," Brian replied. "I'm not positive."

The feeling of hopelessness began to recede. It didn't go away. It merely became less overpowering. Because Tom needed a shave. Because Brian and I did too. Because a piece of orange pulp

162

got stuck between two of my teeth and I didn't have any dental floss. The little problems took over from the big ones.

Normalcy?

Not really. But something akin to it.

We were three men sharing two rooms. The question of who was going to use which bathroom suddenly seemed important. And whether Tom should shave with my safety razor or Brian's electric one. And what we were going to do about a clean shirt for him; mine were too small and Brian's were too large.

Ray and Blanche had been in their graves for less than twenty-four hours. Daisy was missing. Tom was liable to come apart again at any moment. But the big issue was that my brown socks didn't look right with his black shoes.

The three of us went down to the coffee shop for breakfast. On the way, Tom wanted to buy a newspaper. I tried to stop him, but couldn't. There was nothing in it about Daisy, however. And the story of the murders was a mere three inches on page ten. It said little more than that the sheriff's office was continuing its investigation.

Tom ordered crisp bacon but got some that was only half cooked. Brian said that the butter tasted like margarine. I kept staring at an elderly woman who had palsy; watching her attempts to get the cup to her lips without spilling the coffee made me nervous, yet for some reason I couldn't turn my eyes away.

Tom ate the bacon even though it wasn't the way he wanted it. And two poached eggs on toast. And a sweet roll. Furthermore, he smiled. Twice.

At one point he started to speak, changed his mind, then changed it back again. "What's Mutual Claims selling for?" he asked.

Brian had the newspaper. "It closed yesterday at a hundred and thirty-eight," he said. "Unchanged."

That was the extent of our conversation on the items that really mattered.

After breakfast Tom announced that he was going to call

Daisy. I tried to talk him out of it. He insisted. I almost panicked. But when he dialed the number in Great Neck there was no answer.

I told Brian that there was a shopping center a few blocks away, at the intersection of Camelback Road and Scottsdale Road. I suggested that he drive Tom over there to buy the gear he needed.

They left.

I started to call the office but realized that it was Saturday, so I called Mark at home. When I told him about Daisy he was all for rushing to get the next plane to Phoenix. It took five minutes to dissuade him.

Then I called Irving and asked him what information he had on Ray Petacque's telephone calls from New York.

"Zilch," he replied.

"What do you mean, 'Zilch'?"

"I sent Rothland over to the hotel. They wouldn't give him any information."

"They damn well would've given it to Brian," I said angrily. I didn't usually make that kind of remark, comparing one member of my staff unfavorably with another. Nor did I usually lose my temper with Irving.

He didn't know what to make of it. "But, Brock—"

"I don't want any excuses. I want to know about those telephone calls, and if you can't get the information, I'll send Brian back there to do it for you. Understand? I don't care if you have to bribe someone or call the president of the telephone company. I don't care what you do. But I want that information and I want it soon." I slammed down the telephone, felt remorseful, started to call back and apologize, but decided that I had no reason to apologize and went out onto the balcony.

I wasn't there long, however, for within minutes the telephone rang.

It was Ed. He'd been up all night, he said, worrying about Daisy. Did I have any news?

I said that I hadn't.

164

"How's Tom?"

"Considerably better at the moment. I haven't told him about her."

"Can I talk to him?"

"He's not here. Brian's taken him shopping. He can't remember where his stuff is."

"It's in the trunk of my car. Sooner or later you're going to have to tell him about Daisy."

"I know. But I'd rather wait."

He didn't have anything else to say.

And no sooner had I finished talking to him than General Petacque called. The conversation with him was similar to the one with Ed. He too had had a bad night, worrying about Daisy. He too wanted to know how Tom was. I told him that the sheriff's men had begun looking for Daisy and that Tom didn't yet know she was missing. He sounded like a different man from the General Petacque I knew. The arrogance was gone. There could be no doubt that he was deeply troubled.

"Have you talked to Schroeder?" I asked.

"No. I—I wouldn't know what to say to him."

I let it go at that. He seemed to want to continue to talk, but not to have anything further to talk about.

I returned to the balcony. The sun was strong and warm. There was a lounge chair with plastic webbing. I stretched out on it. Something has to happen soon, I thought. Something has to break.

But nothing did.

Nothing at all.

In one way it seemed strange. In another it didn't. The matter of Daisy's disappearance was in the hands of the people who were best equipped to do something about it. The only thing I could handle better than they was the investigation of Mutual Claims. But that had become secondary. And anyway, my hands were tied. Schroeder, I was quite positive, would no longer let me near him. The same with Jackley.

After a while I roused myself to look at the cars parked below, to see if the brown car had come back. It hadn't.

I went into the room to get the newspaper, which Brian had left on the bed, returned to the lounge chair and began to read.

Goldwater's was having a special sale of women's housecoats. A giant tanker had gone aground off the coast of Venezuela, and oil was spilling into the Atlantic in huge quantities. A twenty-two-year-old garage mechanic had been convicted of sexually assaulting an eight-year-old boy. Montgomery Ward was offering forty-pound bags of soil-enriching organic mulch for only $1.99, and juniper plants for only 88¢ each.

But there was something else. An article on the editorial page. It was headed, "ARE WE REALLY WORSE?" It raised the question of whether the rate of crime in Phoenix was really higher than that of other cities. It concluded that, higher or not, the crime rate was a serious problem and that the law-enforcement agencies should be doing more about it. It cited the Petacque murders as an example of how nobody was really safe.

I thought of Harlow and Eames, and of the other men I'd met at the Mesa substation. They wouldn't like that editorial, and I couldn't blame them if they didn't. But it might serve as a goad to them. Perhaps too much of a goad.

Tom and Brian were gone a long time. I began to worry.

It was almost noon when they returned, their arms full of packages.

"It took you long enough," I said.

"We detoured," Tom said. "I met Lee Kelly's widow."

Brian explained that on the way to the shopping center he'd told Tom in detail about our visit to her and about the man who'd supposedly seen her husband's murderer. Tom had insisted on going to her apartment and getting the man's name. "We got there just in the nick of time," he said. "The movers were taking out the last of the boxes. Her plane leaves in a couple of hours." He paused. "It was sad. She was crying."

"Did you get the man's name?" I asked.

166

"Trask," Tom said. "We went to see him. I had that picture in my pocket."

"Was he home?"

"He was home. He's seventy-eight years old and has angina. I don't know, though. I showed him the picture. He couldn't say one way or the other. He'd only caught a glimpse of the man."

"It was more yes than no," Brian added.

Tom looked at me. He seemed disappointed. "I didn't think you'd still be here."

"Where did you think I'd be?"

"Seeing Schroeder, or something."

"I have the feeling that Schroeder is busy this morning. With the detectives who interviewed you."

He raised his eyebrows.

"I talked to them last night. I told them about him."

"Why? They won't be able to get anything out of him."

"Because I thought it was time to."

He was annoyed. I was annoyed too, because part of me felt that he was right. That I really ought to be doing something.

Tom began to unpack his purchases. Then he asked, "Do you happen to know where my father and Clarissa are? I think I ought to go see them."

"I wouldn't do that if I were you," I said. "I've spoken to him. He's all right. Maybe tomorrow."

"Where is he?"

"At the Arizona Biltmore."

"Perhaps you're right. Tomorrow. He's probably mad at me." He shook his head sadly. "That's what he's always been," he said. "Mad at me. At Ray too, most of the time. The only one he ever really liked is Clarissa."

And so the waiting, the idleness went on.

Until one-thirty, when suddenly everything happened at once.

We were having lunch in the coffee shop when a bellboy who couldn't have been more than seventeen years old appeared at the entrance and called out at the top of his voice, "Brockton Potter! Brockton Potter! Telephone!"

I jumped up and hurried over to him. "That's me."

"Long distance."

"Tell the operator I'll take it in my room," I said, and raced off.

The call was from Mark. He sounded shaken. He'd just talked to Daisy's sister, he said. A man from the FBI had been to see her. She was hysterical. She insisted on leaving for Phoenix immediately. Mark hadn't been able to talk her out of it. "She wanted to know where Tom was," he added. "I couldn't tell her I didn't know. I said he was with you."

"I wish you hadn't."

"It didn't seem right not to, Brock."

"Well, what's done is done. Is there anything about Daisy in the newspapers there?"

"Not yet. How about there?"

"Not yet."

"I wanted to warn you, that's all," Mark concluded.

I thanked him and hung up. Now I was going to have to break the news to Tom and I didn't know how.

Another call came through almost immediately. This one was from Daisy's sister. She wanted to talk to Tom. And Mark hadn't exaggerated; she *was* hysterical.

Tom wasn't available, I lied. He was with the police. Then I set to work calming her down. It took a while. I explained that everyone was doing his utmost to locate Daisy, that there were so many people working on the case that they were bound to find her within hours. I pointed out that someone had to stay with Jerry; he'd been shunted about enough. I promised to keep her advised as to everything that was happening.

I eventually succeeded in persuading her to remain in Great Neck.

I started back to the coffee shop, but before I reached the door the telephone rang again.

"Jesus Christ," I said aloud.

"I've been trying to get you for ten minutes," Ed told me irritably, "but your line's been busy. Who were you talking to?"

"New York."

"I wanted to tell you that two men from the FBI were here. They left a little while ago. They had a court order to put some kind of device on my telephone, in case of a ransom demand or something. I think they're planning to do the same thing to your telephone."

"O.K."

"They also want pictures of Daisy. I don't have any. And they'll ask you all kinds of questions."

"O.K."

There was a knock at my door.

"Actually, I expected them sooner," Ed went on, "but they had a hard time finding a judge to sign the order."

"I have to hang up," I said. "Someone's here now."

I put down the telephone and quickly closed the connecting door to Brian's room. Just in case we might once again need two separate rooms.

But it wasn't the FBI men who were knocking. It was Brian and Tom.

"We got worried," Tom explained.

"It was Mark," I said. "Nothing important. Why don't you go back and finish your lunch?"

"We finished it."

I had to get Tom out of the way before the men from the FBI arrived. "Well, I haven't finished mine. Come with me and keep me company."

But as it turned out, there wasn't time. For while we were standing there bickering over a hundred-yard walk to get me half of a meal I didn't even want, the two FBI men did knock on the door.

There was nothing I could do but let them in.

"Mr. Petacque?" one of them inquired.

"No," I said with a sinking feeling. "I'm Mr. Potter. That's Mr. Petacque."

They approached Tom. "Agents Rockland and Cassiday," the spokesman said. "Federal Bureau of Investigation. We'd like to ask you some questions, if we may."

"Sure," Tom said. "I've told the detectives at the sheriff's office all I remember. But if it'll help . . ."

"It will, we hope. And if you have any pictures . . ."

"Pictures?"

"Of your wife."

"My wife?"

"The woman who's been reported missing."

"I don't understand. My wife . . ."

"He doesn't know," I explained. I turned to Tom. "I'm afraid I have some bad news, Tom. Daisy's disappeared."

"No," he whispered. Then he shouted it. "No!" The pupils of his eyes dilated. His voice rose even higher. "No! No! *No!*" He pushed one of the FBI men aside. "I have to find her!" He started for the door.

Brian intercepted him. "Mr. Petacque—"

Tom whirled and lashed out with his fist. The blow caught Brian on the jaw and sent him staggering against the wall.

I dashed over and grabbed Tom from behind. We were evenly matched physically, but at that moment it was as if he outweighed me by a hundred pounds. He flung me off with such force that I too staggered against the wall. He uttered a sob and reached for the doorknob. I recovered and grabbed him again. Brian came to my assistance. Tom took on both of us, sobbing, kicking, elbowing and yelling at us to get out of his way.

The FBI men joined the fray, carefully at first, then, as they felt the irrational, blind fury of the man, in earnest.

Even with four of us trying to hold him back, Tom managed to get the door open. He dragged all four of us out to the corridor. "Let me go!" he kept shouting. "Let me go!"

One of the FBI men got him around the neck and forced him back into the room, but he broke away. He began to swear. Obscenities poured from his mouth. He reached the door again. Brian seized one of his ankles. He pulled his leg away and kicked Brian in the face.

I forced my way between him and the door. He jammed his fist into my stomach. I doubled up and dropped to my knees, gasping for breath. He tried to get around me, but just then one of the FBI men hit him hard on the cheek, and he sagged. Brian got back into the action. I regained my breath. We pinned him against the wall.

"Better get some help," one of the FBI men panted, and the other went to the telephone.

Ten minutes later, Tom was handcuffed. But even then he continued to struggle.

It took four policemen to get him down the steps and into a squad car.

They were taking him to Arizona State Hospital. For psychiatric examination.

– 35 –

Brian's nose was bleeding. One of the FBI men—Cassiday— had a rip in his coat. I ached in half a dozen places.

"It's really my fault," I said. "I should have told him before."

No one disagreed with me.

"How long will they keep him there?" I asked.

"Seems to me," Rockland observed dryly, "they ought to keep him there forever. Does he get like that often?"

I shook my head. "Never. . . . But after all, she *is* his wife."

"I suppose." He cleared his throat. "Well, then, suppose you tell us what *you* know."

I gave them a fifteen-minute rundown. Ray's visit to New York. Tom's experience at Ray's house. His call to Daisy. The brown car that had followed me. My suspicions about Schroeder.

They seemed to be acquainted with most of the facts. They simply listened, their faces grave. When I finished, they volunteered a little information of their own. The sheriff's office had traced the license number of the car, through the Motor Vehicle Division. The license number I'd given them was registered in the name of one Felipe Valdez, who'd reported his car stolen on Monday from in front of his house on Third Street. But Valdez's car wasn't brown and wasn't a sedan. It was possible that two cars had been stolen, and the license plates of one had been put on the other. Or that the brown car actually belonged to one of the men who'd been riding in it and that Valdez's car had been abandoned somewhere. In any case, it was likely that the license plates had been switched since I'd last seen the car. More than once, perhaps.

"What about the picture Tom came up with?" I asked. "One of the detectives was going to take it over to the Immigration and Naturalization people."

"We wouldn't know about that," Cassiday said.

"That's a different department," said Rockland.

They said it too quickly. I didn't believe them.

"And we're only working on the kidnapping case," Rockland added. "If that's what it is. We still don't know that Mrs. Petacque didn't disappear voluntarily."

I didn't believe that either. Daisy's disappearance and the two murders were part of the same case, and they knew it. "Did you find out whether she actually left New York?" I asked.

"Yes," Rockland admitted with some reluctance. "We found her name on a passenger list. She arrived here, all right. But what happened after that we don't know. Now, we have a court order here—"

"What about Schroeder?"

Their faces went blank. There was a silence. "We ourselves haven't talked to him," Cassiday said finally. "We only got assigned to the case this morning."

"Has anyone else talked to him?"

"We wouldn't know. Now, about this court order." Cassiday explained about monitoring my calls.

I didn't think they'd accomplish anything by it. Furthermore, it would be a nuisance. But I said, "Go ahead."

"What about my phone?" Brian asked.

"We didn't know about you," Rockland admitted.

"Your phone will be disconnected," Cassiday said.

"Excuse me," I said. "I need a drink. Can I buy you fellows one?"

They said no. I felt pretty shaky, I said; did they mind if I made a quick trip to the bar? Cassiday replied that they weren't finished with me. I glanced at my watch. Twenty minutes to three. In New York, twenty minutes to five. I'd only be gone a few minutes, I said; meanwhile they could work on the telephone, if that was what they wanted to do. Go ahead, then, Cassiday conceded.

I got myself out of the room before either of them could change his mind.

There were pay telephones in the corridor between the lobby and the coffee shop. I picked up one of them and dialed the operator. I told her that I wanted to make a person-to-person call to a lawyer in New York whose name was Evelyn Natwick, that it was an emergency call.

The next three minutes were bad. The operator insisted that,

173

emergency or no emergency, she couldn't give me the number; I had to dial New York Information. I dialed it. The New York Information operator thought I said "Matwick" and couldn't find the number. Then, when we got the spelling straightened out, I discovered that I didn't have enough change in my pocket and had to leave the telephone dangling on its cord while I went to the cashier's window.

But Evelyn Natwick was, luckily, at home.

"I have a case for you," I said.

"It's Saturday," she said.

"This is honest-to-God urgent," I said. "Don't worry about your fee. Whatever it is, I'll pay it. But I need action this afternoon. I'm in Scottsdale, Arizona. Friends of mine were murdered here a few days ago."

"Good heavens!"

"Just listen, Evelyn. Listen carefully." I told her about the sketch Tom had worked on with the police artist. I said that the detectives from the sheriff's office in Mesa were going to try to get someone at the INS in Phoenix to make an identification. I wanted to know whether they'd done so and what steps could be taken if they hadn't.

"The people in INS aren't exactly friends of mine, Brock. I spend most of my time fighting them."

"You must have contacts, though. If not in New York, then in Washington. I don't care what you have to do, Evelyn—I need to know."

"I do, but it's impossible, Brock. It's *Saturday.*"

"Nothing is impossible, Evelyn. Ever."

After a brief silence she said, "I suppose I could contact one of the Phoenix immigration lawyers at home. I've had dealings with a couple of them. What, precisely, are you trying to find out?"

I gave her the details.

"I'll see what I can do," she agreed. "Where can I get in touch with you?"

"You can't. The FBI is monitoring my calls. I'll have to get in touch with you. Please don't leave your apartment until you hear from me, Evelyn. Did you have plans for tonight?"

"Yes, but that doesn't matter. Business first."

"Good girl. Thank you. Thank you very much. It may be hours before I'm free to call again, but wait. Please."

I hung up. Then I did go to the bar.

I ordered a double Scotch. And drank it in three gulps.

– 36 –

The FBI men were in no hurry. After they got the telephone doctored, they took me through my story again. This time they asked questions. It was obvious that they were hoping to find inconsistencies. They didn't find them. Yet the second time around, my story didn't sound good, even to me.

Ed, Tom, myself—we'd all behaved irrationally. During periods of stress, it seemed to me, everyone behaves irrationally—and I said so. But the very fact that I had to say it provoked doubts. In Tom's case the irrationality was something they'd seen in action and could understand. Even Ed's actions were explainable: he'd had a very disturbed man on his hands and had done what seemed right to him at the moment. It was my own performance that made the least sense. Why hadn't I turned the case over to the authorities immediately? Why hadn't I reported the fact that I was being followed? What had I been trying to cover up?

I hadn't been trying to cover up anything, I said. I'd merely been trying to do two jobs at the same time—find Tom and learn what was wrong at Mutual Claims—and to do them in my own way.

Cassiday and Rockland remained skeptical. But, in all fairness, I had to admit that it would have been difficult for anyone interviewing me in that motel room, listening to my account of what

175

I'd done since arriving in Phoenix, to be anything other than skeptical. Schroeder had been in New York at the time Ray and Blanche were murdered. He probably had an equally good alibi for the time of Kelly's murder. I had no proof that anything was amiss at Mutual Claims. No one had any proof that Daisy had been kidnapped; she'd simply got off a plane in Phoenix and not been seen since.

All they said, finally, was let's take one thing at a time. If Mrs. Petacque has been kidnapped, let's get her back. Then let's get her story. But, in passing, they added that conspiracy to commit murder is a difficult charge to prove unless you catch the person who did the actual killing and he testifies against the person who put him up to it.

To which I added, silently, that fraud was also a difficult charge to prove, without the cooperation one of the participants in the fraud.

It was after six o'clock when they left. They said that someone from their office would be in touch with me. Meanwhile, if anyone did contact me about Daisy by telephone, they'd get the message at the same time I did. They'd know immediately where the call came from and make a voice print of whoever was talking.

"And suppose I'm contacted some other way?" I asked.

"Let us know at once," Rockland said. He told me what number to call. Someone was on duty all the time, and everyone in the office had been alerted.

I went out onto the balcony and waited until they drove away. Then I hurried to the pay phone off the lobby and called Evelyn Natwick.

She had information for me. More than I'd dared hope for.

The man in the artist's sketch had indeed been identified. By no less an authority than the assistant district director for investigation at the Phoenix office of the Immigration and Naturalization Service. With certainty. With gratitude. With jubilation. As Juan Manuel Barrios.

Barrios had been deported to Mexico as an illegal alien two and a half times—the half being a deportation that hadn't come off. It hadn't come off because Barrios had shot the immigration officer who was picking him up, and escaped. The immigration officer hadn't died; he'd merely been crippled for life.

There wasn't a single person in the Phoenix office of the INS who didn't know about the Barrios case. There wasn't an investigator among them who didn't hope that someday he personally would encounter Barrios and bring him in. Except that this time Barrios wouldn't be deported. He'd be brought to trial and sent to jail.

And because of the shooting, Barrios wasn't solely the concern of the INS. The FBI was also interested; pictures of him taken at the time of his previous deportations and facsimiles of his fingerprints were on file in Washington. The Phoenix Police Department was likewise interested, as was the Maricopa County sheriff's office.

Detective Harlow wouldn't have had to go to the INS if anyone at the Mesa substation had associated the name with the face, but no one had. As soon as the assistant district director gave him the name, however, he remembered the case and telephoned the information to Mesa. Even Harvey Magill, the Phoenix lawyer from whom Evelyn had got her information, was familiar with the Barrios case. He knew the investigator who'd been crippled, and personally hoped that Barrios would be caught. Several investigators, he'd learned, had volunteered to give up their weekend in order to mount a search.

I could safely assume, Evelyn said, that word had gone out to the top echelons at the police department, the sheriff's office and the FBI that Barrios had been seen in Paradise Valley on Monday night, was wanted for questioning in connection with the Petacque murders and was possibly implicated in the disappearance of Mrs. Daisy Petacque. All agencies would be on the lookout for Juan Manuel Barrios.

"How long ago did he shoot that investigator?" I asked.

"Ten months."

"So for ten months they've been chasing him and for ten months they haven't been able to locate him."

"They didn't know he was still in Arizona. They thought he'd skipped to a different part of the country altogether. That's my guess, at any rate. And you have no idea what they're up against, Brock. I'm constantly fighting them, but I do understand their problems. There are literally millions of illegal aliens in this country, coming and going quite freely, getting jobs here, there and everywhere. It's possible for one of them to disappear from Arizona, turn up in Idaho, disappear from Idaho, turn up in New Jersey, disappear from New Jersey and not turn up at all."

"I've heard all about that, but it doesn't solve the immediate problem."

"Well, that's the way it is. As far as the immediate problem is concerned, I don't know what will solve it. But I can tell you this. The INS may not have located Barrios yet, but they have a sizable file on him, which will certainly help."

"Were you able to find out what's in the file?"

"Not really. They wouldn't give information like that to someone like Harvey. But a few things are common knowledge. They were in the newspapers at the time, Harvey said. The first time Barrios was picked up, he was a contract laborer, picking oranges. The second time, he was working on a construction job in downtown Phoenix. The third time, the time he shot that man, he was

178

also working on a construction job. The INS, and whoever they share the information with, undoubtedly knows quite a bit about where he worked, where he lived, who his friends were. Also about his family and background in Mexico."

If, with all that information, they hadn't been able to find him before, would they be able to find him now? I was skeptical. That wasn't Evelyn's concern, however. She'd done what I'd asked her to do and done it well. "I can't tell you how much I appreciate all this," I said. "When I get back to New York I'm going to buy you the best dinner in town. Meanwhile send your bill to the office."

"The dinner I'll accept, but you can forget about a bill."

"Don't be ridiculous, Evelyn."

"No. I have enough trouble with my conscience at times. This one is on the house. And good luck."

We hung up, and I stood there, my hand on the ledge under the telephone. Juan Manuel Barrios, I thought, a man with nothing to lose.

Evidently Steve Schroeder was not only talented in devising programs for computers. He was also talented in hiring the most suitable people to do whatever he wanted done.

– 38 –

Brian was leaning against the desk, frowning. He said, "Mr. Silvers called." Then he came over to me. He pointed at the telephone. "Does that thing pick up everything we say?" he whispered in my ear.

"I don't know," I whispered back. I hadn't thought to ask the FBI men whether the device they'd attached to our telephone picked up only telephone conversations or all sounds in the room.

Brian led me out onto the balcony and closed the sliding glass door behind us. "I thought he might say something that you

179

wouldn't want them to hear and I tried to cut him off. I said you'd call him back, but he said you couldn't—he was in a phone booth at the airport in Winston-Salem, North Carolina, and his plane was about to take off; he was on his way back to New York."

"Winston-Salem, North Carolina?"

"He said he had some telephone numbers for you. He said he had a hard time getting them. He had to find out who owned the hotel, since it wasn't a chain. Then the owner turned out to be someone who lived in Winston-Salem and wouldn't cooperate. So Mr. Silvers decided to go down to Winston-Salem and talk to him in person."

I smiled. "What a guy!"

"At any rate, I wrote down the information." He handed me a piece of paper.

Ray had made three long-distance calls. All of them to Phoenix. Two to one number, one to another.

I went into the room and opened the telephone directory. I wasn't surprised by what I found. The two calls had been to Ray's home number. The other had been to Schroeder's.

We returned to the balcony. I told Brian what I thought. "The trouble with Ray was, he just wasn't smart. He tried to put pressure on Schroeder. He underestimated the man."

"You mean he told Schroeder what he was doing in New York?"

I nodded. "Threatened him, probably."

"That *was* dumb."

"Sure. But understandable in a way. He must have had doubts about Tom. He wasn't certain that Tom would be able to accomplish more with Schroeder than he himself had. And he was naïve enough to believe that, threatened with exposure, Schroeder would break down and confess everything."

"But he knew that Schroeder had had Kelly killed—for much less."

"He didn't know; he merely had a strong suspicion. And even so, he must have felt that he personally was safe, that Schroeder

180

would never do a thing like that to him. That's why I say he underestimated the man."

"He left Schroeder no choice."

"I wouldn't say that. There's always a choice. But he did put Schroeder in a bad spot, and being the kind of man he was, Schroeder decided to fight his way out of it by hiring Barrios to kill Ray and by coming to New York himself to discredit Ray and at the same time to warn Tom—or, as it turned out, me—that any attempt to expose Mutual Claims would have serious consequences for Price, Potter and Petacque."

"Barrios?"

I told him about my conversations with Evelyn Natwick.

He gazed into the distance. Lights were beginning to appear in the houses on Camelback Mountain. "A construction worker," he said after a while. "It fits. Schroeder is hung up on real estate. He probably went out every day to inspect the projects he was having built. He would have gotten to know some of the workers."

"And he would have hired contractors who used cheap labor."

"Are you going to tell the FBI?"

"Tell them what?"

"About the telephone call Mr. Petacque's brother made to Schroeder."

"They already know about it from listening in on Irving's call. But the fact that Ray called Schroeder doesn't prove anything, or wouldn't to them. And they know all about Barrios—they've known about him all day." I paused. "No, I'm sure the FBI and the sheriff's office and the INS and God knows who else are doing all they can. I'm worried about Tom, though. He doesn't belong in that hospital. He isn't crazy."

"He's safe there, though."

"Yes. But it isn't going to do him any good to be there. I'm going to call his New York doctor and ask him to see what he can do to get him out."

We went back into the room and I placed the call. Dr. Balter had left his office, the woman at his answering service said; he could be reached at home. She gave me his home number, and I tried it. Balter answered the telephone himself.

"Good Lord!" he exclaimed after I told him what had happened.

"Can you come out here?" I asked.

"I wish I could, but I can't. I have a full schedule, and two of my patients are having crises. But I'll get in touch with someone local."

"Who?"

"I don't know. I'll have to make some inquiries."

I pictured him sitting with the telephone in one hand, a cigar in the other. I also pictured a man with earphones, listening to what we were saying. And a recording machine, its reels spinning slowly, picking up every word.

Balter said he'd go to work on the problem immediately. He didn't think he'd have any difficulty in locating a competent doctor, but he did believe that the doctor wouldn't be able to accomplish anything for at least a day. He'd keep me posted.

The image of the recording machine, the spinning reels, remained with me after the call was completed. The danger of a device like that. The power. The uses to which it could be put. "Brian," I said, "first thing in the morning I want you to go out and find a place that's open and buy us a recorder. The smallest and best you can find. One that records and plays back."

Brian frowned. Then smiled. Then nodded.

It was, I estimated, twenty or twenty-two hours since Daisy's plane had landed. Soon someone would make a move.

I tried to anticipate what the move would be, to prepare for it.

"Hungry?" Brian asked presently.

"No," I replied. "But you go ahead and have dinner."

"What are you going to do?"

"Sit here and wait."

He settled back in his chair.

"Go ahead," I urged. "Get something to eat."

"I'll stay with you."

We lapsed into silence, and time passed. I no longer had the feeling that I should be doing something. I knew that the inactivity, the waiting, was a necessary part of the game. It had to be endured. And before long it would end. I was certain of that.

The thought of Daisy caused an ache deep inside me. She'd done nothing wrong, yet she was being made to suffer.

My thoughts drifted to Ray and Blanche. It was too late to do anything for them. But they hadn't deserved to die.

Neither had Lee Kelly.

The last of the day's sunlight disappeared. Brian turned on a lamp.

A population boom. Soaring land values. Profits to reinvest. A belief that the boom would go on forever, that it was impossible to lose. Optimism. False optimism.

A tree doesn't grow to heaven. Because someone didn't realize that, three people were dead.

The telephone rang. I answered it. Ed Avery wanted to know whether I'd heard anything about Daisy. I told him I hadn't. He said he hadn't either.

I went back to my chair.

How much longer?

No way of knowing.

Brian turned on another lamp.

We continued to wait.

Then it happened. The telephone rang again. And this time it was the call I'd been expecting. Except that instead of coming from Steve Schroeder, it came from Frank Jackley.

He phrased it carefully. As if he knew that a third party was listening. As if I were an old friend, a neighbor. "Maggie and Chuck've gone out," he said. "I'm alone. How about dropping over for a drink?"

"Has something come up?" I asked.

It didn't work. He simply said, "I have a well-stocked bar. With everything you want."

I had to accept, and both of us knew it. "All right," I said. He hung up.

"Jackley wants me to come to his house," I told Brian.

Brian pointed to the telephone with one hand and cupped the other to his ear.

I nodded.

"You're going?" Brian asked.

"How could I refuse?"

"I'll go with you."

I shrugged.

We left the room. As soon as we were in the corridor, I said, "You're not going with me. I'm in no danger. They need me. And there's something else I want you to do, something more important. How good are you at breaking and entering?"

His eyes widened.

"I want you to break into Ray Petacque's house. Tonight. I don't want you to take anything except a key to the front or back door, if you can find one. If not, then leave one of the doors open. One way or another, I want to be able to get into the house tomorrow. If you can't fix one of the doors so that it'll be unlocked, then leave a window open. Think you can do it?"

Brian grinned and nodded.

I gave him the address, and we went down to our cars.

The Rolls wasn't in the driveway, and the front of the house was dark. I walked around to the back. The family room was lit up. Jackley was sitting with his back to the window. He was alone. I returned to the front of the house and rang the bell. A moment later the door opened.

"I'm here," I said.

Instead of inviting me in, he stepped outside. "Actually," he said, "I'm not the one who wants to see you. Steve is."

"That's what I figured," I said.

"I'll walk you over there."

"No need. I can find the house."

"Suit yourself." He went back inside and closed the door.

I crossed the yard to the street. Their plan had worked. No one had followed me.

I left my car where it was and walked.

Schroeder's house was more brightly lit. I took a deep breath and lifted the heavy brass knocker. It fell with a resounding clunk.

Schroeder offered no greeting. He merely nodded and stepped aside to let me in.

The interior was exactly as I remembered it. A large foyer with a floor of blue-and-white tile and several arched doorways framed in the same blue-and-white tile. A long oak table holding a Chinese vase filled with artificial flowers stood against one wall. Schroeder hadn't changed a thing.

I started toward the living room, but Schroeder said, "This way," and led me past it, through one of the smaller arches and along a corridor that connected the foyer with the back of the house. He opened a leaded glass door and walked across a flagstone terrace. I followed him.

The swimming pool was illuminated by underwater lights, but either he'd removed the spotlights, which, I recalled, lit up the date palms that dotted the back yard, or else he hadn't turned them on, for the rest of the yard was quite dark.

"Where are we going?" I asked.

185

"The golf course."

I hesitated. The golf course would be deserted. Then I walked on. He wouldn't dare, I thought.

A tall hedge separated his property from the golf course. We moved cautiously along it, Schroeder in the lead, until we came to the break at the end. "Watch out for the branches," he said, pushing some aside.

The back yard had been dimly lit by the glow from the back windows of the house and from the swimming pool, but the golf course was almost pitch dark. Schroeder slowed his pace, as if he himself wasn't sure where we were going. He said nothing, however. I stayed close behind him and asked no questions. It was his show. We crossed some stubby grass, which pulled at the legs of my pants, then the going was easier. We'd emerged from the rough onto one of the fairways, I guessed. Schroeder was no more than a vague outline.

We walked for perhaps fifty yards and climbed a slight rise. The ground at one side of the rise was light in color. A sand trap. At the top of the rise Schroeder swore and took a step backward, bumping into me. And at the same moment I felt a spray of water. We were at the edge of one of the greens, and a sprinkler was going.

"O.K.," he said. "This is far enough. Now I'll tell you what you're going to do."

"What am I going to do?" I could scarcely see him.

"You're going to buy some stock." He sounded weary, like a man at the end of his tether.

"I am?"

"Yes." He sighed. "You've caused me a lot of trouble today."

"Is that so?"

"Two hours with the FBI, an hour and a half with a couple of detectives from the sheriff's office."

Which explained why we were on the golf course instead of inside the house, I guessed. Schroeder was taking no chances on being overheard, electronically or otherwise.

186

"I figure they came because of something you told them."

"No kidding?"

"So you're going to buy some stock."

"What stock am I going to buy?"

"Mutual Claims. Not just you. Your partners are going to buy some too. You're going to buy ten thousand shares apiece. In your own names. Through a brokerage house in Los Angeles."

"And then?"

"And then you're going to send out a letter, predicting record earnings for Mutual Claims.

"Which will drive the price up."

"Right. Each of you will make a nice little profit."

"Except that I've just sent out a letter recommending that the stock be sold. . . . It'd look like we deliberately forced the price down so that we could buy it cheap and make those nice little profits at the expense of our customers. If our customers didn't put us out of business after that, the SEC would. We might even go to jail."

"That's your problem."

"I'd be destroying every shred of credibility I ever had."

"Possibly."

"And of course no one would ever believe any charges I leveled at Mutual Claims or at you."

"Hardly."

"And suppose I refuse."

Schroeder took some time before answering. A gust of wind swept across the golf course. Spray from the sprinkler landed on my forehead. "The FBI," he said finally, "think I know something about Tom's wife. It seems she's disappeared."

I said nothing.

"I told them how ridiculous it was to think that I'd know anything about it. They seemed to believe me. But I guess she really has disappeared. Don't you agree?"

"Yes," I said. "She's disappeared."

"I'd hate to see anything happen to her. It could, though, if you refused."

"What assurance do I have that if I do as you say Daisy will be released?"

"We all have to take chances at times."

If he was the one who'd met Daisy at the airport, he couldn't possibly allow her to be released. Not ever. And I was reasonably certain that he was indeed the one who had met her at the airport. She wouldn't have gone with anyone she didn't know. "Of course," I said, "I do have something in my favor that you probably aren't aware of. I have a tape recording of a telephone conversation that Ray Petacque made to you from his hotel in New York. And one of a conversation that took place between him and Tom at Tom's apartment last Saturday night. Those two conversations, taken together, make it pretty clear that Lee Kelly was killed on your instructions. And a good prosecuting attorney could make an excellent case from them that you had reason to order Barrios to kill Ray too. So far I haven't mentioned those tapes to the sheriff's men, but if Daisy isn't released unharmed I'll have no choice."

There was a long silence. I used it to pray.

The silence continued.

I finished my prayer. I said, "It will be kind of like Ray's coming back from the grave to haunt you."

My prayer was answered. "Why would Ray make recordings?" Schroeder asked.

"To build a case against you and vindicate himself. . . . And I know where they are."

"What do you have in mind?" Schroeder asked.

"A simple deal. You bring Daisy to me unharmed, and I'll turn the two tapes over to you. I'll also promise to drop any investigation into Mutual Claims. We'll let nature take its course."

"How do I know there aren't copies of the tapes? How do I know you'll keep your word?"

188

"You said it yourself, Steve. We all have to take chances at times."

We made arrangements for the exchange. Or at least we went through the motions.

It was eleven o'clock when I returned to the motel.

Brian wasn't there.

– 40 –

But the message light on the base of the telephone was flashing. I dialed the operator. Dr. Balter had called and wanted me to call him back.

I did. He said that a Dr. George Champion had been recommended to him. He'd spoken to Champion, who'd agreed to contact someone on the staff of Arizona State Hospital first thing in the morning and to see Tom sometime during the day.

"Any news of his wife?" he asked.

"Nothing definite," I replied.

He groaned and asked me to keep him posted. Then he hung up.

Brian didn't return until a quarter to twelve. He looked dusty and disheveled. A flashlight protruded from the waistband of his slacks.

I pushed him back into the corridor and closed the door. "Did you do it?"

"Yes. But it took me an hour to find the house. And I got lost again on the way back. What about you?"

"Let's have a drink."

"Couldn't we have something to eat instead?"

We went down to his car and cruised around until we found a drive-in that was open. Brian explained that the first thing he'd done was look for a discount store that kept late hours. He'd found one, bought the flashlight, some masking tape to narrow its beam, and a chisel. But since he hadn't been able to get the item he needed most—a glass cutter—he'd had to break a window. The shattering glass had made such a racket that he'd panicked—jumped into his car and driven away. But evidently no one had heard the noise, for when he'd returned, cautiously, half an hour later, the place was deserted. He'd opened the broken window, climbed into the house, unlocked a door that connected the sunroom with the back patio and got the hell away from the place as fast as he could.

I described my meeting with Schroeder. Brian was astonished by Schroeder's scheme to discredit Price, Potter and Petacque. And by the fact that Schroeder had believed my story about the tapes.

"I don't know whether he believed it or not," I said. "It's possible that he really didn't. But he can't afford to take any chances. I think, for all his cool, he's pretty shaky by now. He doesn't know what to believe and what not to believe. He's been questioned by the sheriff's men and the FBI, I'm on his tail—he can't quite cope with everything at once. Bringing Daisy out here was the act of a man who's desperate, who's willing to try anything. Now he almost has to kill her to keep her from identifying him."

"Then . . . ?"

"Because I'm desperate too, Brian."

He finished his milk shake and put the empty container on the tray. He sat there, staring out over the steering wheel. "What will you give him instead of the tapes?"

"If I'm lucky, I won't have to give him anything. But you'll pick up a couple of blanks tomorrow when you buy the recorder."

"Why did you pick the Petacque house, though? Of all places."

"Because it seemed logical that Ray would have had the tapes in his possession and hid them, and that he'd have hid them somewhere in the house. And that he'd have told Tom where they were, and that Tom would've told me."

190

"Isn't that stretching things, though?"

"Sure. He didn't want to meet me there. He wanted me to bring the tapes to his house. I refused. And when I said he should come to my room at the motel instead, he refused."

"But if anyone notices the broken window, the place might be under police surveillance."

"The place *is* going to be under police surveillance. You don't think I'm going to tackle this by myself, do you?"

He looked at me. The blinking red light from the window of the service area gave him the appearance of being alternately flushed and pale.

"Brian," I said, "there may not be any tapes of the conversation between Ray and Schroeder or of what Ray and Tom said to each other at Tom's apartment, but there is going to be a tape of the conversation between Schroeder and me tomorrow. And that's what I'm going to use to nail him with. I got the idea back at the motel from the bug the FBI put on my telephone."

"Suppose he won't talk."

"I'll do most of the talking. He'll respond. He won't have to say very much. A few words ought to do it. And I believe I'm good enough at that kind of thing to get him to say those words. That's the other reason I chose Ray's house. Schroeder is less likely to suspect a bug there than anyplace else I could think of."

Brian put his hands on the steering wheel. They too went alternately pink and white. "What about the police?"

"They'll close in when I give the signal."

The waitress came to detach the tray from the side of the car. I paid her. We continued to sit there. We were the only customers.

"This is the way it will work," I said. "There are plenty of stores open on Sunday. We'll pick up the recorder first thing in the morning, then drive over to the Petacque house. I'll get the recorder placed. A desk drawer would be best, I think. You'll drive away. When Schroeder comes, he won't see any cars. I'll be alone in the house. What happens after that is up to me. But I think

I can handle it all right. Then, when I get him to admit that Mutual Claims has been keeping two sets of books, I'll give a signal and the police will arrive—the sheriff's men and the FBI."

Brian was unconvinced. "You're counting on everything happening just the way you want it to. Suppose it doesn't? Suppose Schroeder has Barrios with him, or Barrios and the other guy? Suppose you can't get him into the room where the recorder is? Or the police don't get the signal?"

Those were all very real possibilities, and I knew it. Yet I was annoyed. "Do you have any better ideas?" I asked sharply. "Come on, let's get back to the motel. I want to get in touch with Cassiday and Rockland. This is going to take some organization on their part too."

"And if they don't like the idea? If they'd rather handle things themselves?"

"We'll cross that bridge when we come to it. Let's go, damn it."

Brian started the engine and we left the drive-in. It was after one o'clock, and there was practically no traffic. My mind was racing now. The objections Brian had raised were valid ones. There were plenty of other objections too, and I considered them. Even though I knew that it was a foolish exercise. For in the end a great deal would depend upon luck. So far Schroeder's luck had held but it had to run out sometime. He couldn't continue to win every round.

Motive. That was the key to everything. Team after team of investigators could hammer away at him, but if they couldn't prove that he'd had reason to have Lee Kelly killed, he'd eventually get away with everything. For the Petacque murders had resulted from Kelly's. Daisy's kidnapping too.

It was so simple, really. A few words were all I needed.

He was rattled, and people who are rattled make mistakes.

I'd be doing what I'd been doing for years, what I was best at: using information I already had to gain additional information.

192

The interview began to take shape in my mind. Schroeder's flaws were vanity and self-deception. I'd play to them. . . . You've won, Schroeder. This is what I know, but I can't use it. Right, Schroeder?

Schroeder would implicate Jackley.

And the concealed tape recorder would pick up his words.

What about Barrios, though?

That would depend.

One thing at a time. Schroeder first.

We approached the motel. Brian slowed the car and guided it between the gateposts. For the first time since we left the drive-in, he spoke. "I hope you're right," he said.

"So do I," I said.

He found a parking space under our balcony. We got out of the car.

"You're going to call the FBI men now?" he asked.

"Yes," I said.

We walked along the shrubbery to the short arcade from which a stairway led to the second floor. We turned into it. Brian was ahead of me. The only sounds were the scraping of our shoes on the concrete.

But suddenly an arm closed around my throat and the muzzle of a gun dug into the small of my back.

"You come," a voice said.

– 41 –

Brian heard. He spun around. His lips parted. His nostrils flared. He spread his arms and bent his knees, as if to leap. And froze in that position. For another man brushed past me and pointed a gun at Brian's face.

"You too," he said.

The arm tightened around my throat. I took a step backward. Then a second step. The gun remained pressed against the small of my back.

The other man motioned with his free hand for Brian to follow. Brian remained frozen in his half crouch for a moment, eyeing the gun that was aimed at him, then relaxed and gave a barely perceptible nod of his head. The four of us moved out of the passageway toward the parking lot.

The man behind me whistled once. An automobile engine came to life. Tires hissed on the pavement. A car backed from its parking stall. It pulled up in front of us. There were two men in it, the driver and a passenger in the back seat. The driver reached across and opened the front door. The other man opened the back door.

The arm released me, and the gun directed me toward the back seat. I got into the car. The man who'd had his arm around my throat got in after me, keeping the gun pointed at my head and closing the door without taking his eyes off me. Brian, prodded by the fourth man, climbed into the front seat.

The front door closed. The car moved forward. Wedged between the two men in the back seat, I felt the muzzle of the gun against the skin at the back of my jaw, under the ear. The hand holding the gun was very steady. I stared straight ahead. I felt very cold. Yet I was beginning to sweat.

The man on Brian's right placed the muzzle of his gun under Brian's ear. Our two captors hadn't exchanged a single word, but they seemed to know what to do without speaking, without even looking at each other. They were men who'd worked together before.

The car passed under the portico of the motel and through the gateposts, turning west on Indian School Road, then north on Sixty-eighth Street. A pair of red taillights showed a car also going north, a couple of hundred yards ahead. It was the only other car on the street; there was no southbound traffic whatsoever. And presently the other car turned onto a side street and disappeared from view.

Except for the sound of whirring tires, it was utterly silent. The long, low apartment buildings and one-story houses that lined the street were dark. The driver kept a steady, moderate speed and seemed to know exactly where he was going.

My thoughts remained locked around the single idea: We're going to die; they're going to take us out into the desert and kill us.

The driver slowed the car and made a left turn. I recognized Camelback Road. We traveled a few blocks, then turned right into a less traveled road. I saw the street sign: Invergordon Road. Moments later another sign appeared. It said "VALLEY COUNTRY CLUB." We passed it and kept going. Our direction was north. North toward Camelback Mountain, toward the less populated suburbs, toward the desert.

I was sweating more freely now. Yet the feeling of being cold persisted.

Another left turn. Another right turn. My sense of direction held. We were going alternately north and west. But I had no sense of place. There were no familiar landmarks. I knew I'd been through the area before, but I didn't know when or with whom or what it looked like.

My eyes focused on the back of Brian's head, and suddenly I felt a deep sadness. He was so young, so eager to prove himself. He would have succeeded too. He would have had a fine career. Now the promise would never be fulfilled, the potential would never be realized.

Daisy would die too. Because Schroeder no longer needed her, and because, like the rest of us, she was a threat.

The sheriff's men would question him. So would the FBI. They might even hold him for a few days, or until his lawyers could get him released. But they would never be able to prove that he was responsible for the deaths of six people.

Without turning my head, I tried to see the man who was holding the gun to me, but I couldn't. I felt quite certain, though, that either he or the man in the front seat was Barrios.

Tom had seen only two men at Ray's house, but there'd probably been four. And two of them had been detailed to follow me the day after my arrival. I wondered whether Brian recognized any of the four. Chances were, he did.

Schroeder didn't care about the tapes. Possibly he'd guessed that I was bluffing.

Would it have been better if I'd agreed to buy the stock? Perhaps. That was my big mistake: trying to outwit him. You don't outwit men like Schroeder.

Unless he still hoped to get the tapes.

We passed a sign that I recognized. "PARADISE VALLEY COUNTRY CLUB." I'd been there. With Ray Petacque. It was less than a mile from his house.

It wouldn't make any difference. They'd kill us anyway. I cleared my throat. The muzzle of the gun was shoved deeper into the skin of my neck. It hurt. I moved my head.

The driver slowed the car, then brought it to a complete stop opposite a pair of gateposts. The sign on one of the gateposts said "PARADISE VALLEY COUNTRY ESTATES."

Schroeder wanted the tapes, after all.

The driver guided the car between the gateposts and along the winding incline of Moonlight Way. No one said a word, but I knew that we were on a street that was familiar to all of us.

And presently we were pulling up in front of a house that was likewise familiar to all of us. The car stopped.

"You come," said the man on my right. He shifted the gun to his left hand and reached back with his other hand to open the door. As the door opened, two small lights went on. I saw the gunman's face. He was Barrios.

Keeping the gun pointed at me, he backed cautiously out of the car. I followed him.

The driver said a few words in Spanish. Barrios hesitated, then replied. His reply was also in Spanish. Their exchange evidently referred to Brian, for after Barrios spoke, the front door opened and Brian's captor eased himself out of the car, directing Brian to get out too.

Barrios put the muzzle of the gun to my neck and said, "Go."

196

I started up the driveway, with him behind me. Additional footsteps indicated that Brian and the other man were also coming. There was no moon, but the stars were bright. The house at the end of the driveway was sharply silhouetted.

I heard the car doors close, the car move away. I tried to turn around, but Barrios poked me in the neck with the gun and gave me a shove with his hand. I continued up the driveway. He used the gun to guide me to the front door. When we came to it he reached around me and turned the knob. The door opened.

I stepped into the foyer. The house was in total darkness. The gun prodded me forward. Someone quietly closed the door behind us. I took two uncertain steps and suddenly was blinded by the beam of a light which was aimed right at my eyes.

"Good," said Schroeder.

"The other was with him," Barrios explained.

"Who's your friend?" Schroeder asked me.

"Brian Barth," I said, blinking rapidly. I couldn't see a thing. "Move the light."

Schroeder obliged, and said, "Where are the tapes?"

The beam of his flashlight was directed at the floor. It made a wide circle of light on the carpet and illuminated our shoes, Schroeder's and mine. I still couldn't see his face. "In my motel room," I said. "I was going to bring them over tomorrow."

"Did you search the room?" he asked Barrios.

"*Sí*," Barrios replied. "With Marco. No tapes."

"Potter," Schroeder said slowly, a distinct note of menace in his voice, "I want the tapes."

"Where's Daisy?" I said.

Still speaking slowly, he said, "I want those tapes."

"There are no tapes," I said.

The light seemed to swing in all directions at once, and I felt an excruciating pain as something hard slammed against the bridge of my nose. I yelled and put my hands to my face. My knees turned to rubber. I staggered. Barrios grabbed me around the waist. Schroeder swung the flashlight again. It caught me on the forehead. I groaned and sagged against Barrios.

197

"Where are the tapes?" Schroeder asked.

I tried to say that there were no tapes, but the pain was so bad that I couldn't speak. I was sure my nose was broken and I could feel the blood wetting my hands. No tapes, I thought. No tapes, no tapes, no tapes. But the words wouldn't come.

"In the bathroom," Brian said.

"Get them," Schroeder ordered. "Go with him, Marco."

"Need light," Marco said.

Schroeder played the beam of the flashlight over Brian. "He has a light," he said to Marco. "Let him use it."

"Windows," said Barrios.

"It's O.K.," Schroeder said. "I've closed the drapes."

My nose was starting to swell, and a lump was forming on my forehead. I lowered my hands. Blood trickled onto my upper lip. Words formed in my mind. I tried to get them out. Only one emerged. "Tapes."

I tried again. This time two emerged. "Tapes," I said. "Bedroom."

"Bathroom," Brian said. "I moved them."

"Bedroom," I insisted.

It worked. "Bring him too," Schroeder told Barrios. And to Brian he said, "Show us where."

A second beam appeared as Brian turned on his flashlight. He started across the foyer, pointing the light straight ahead to brighten as wide an area as possible. Marco followed close behind with the gun.

Barrios, still holding me around the waist, kept the gun at the back of my neck. He gave me a push. I took a step, faltered, but managed to remain upright. Barrios removed his arm from my waist and nudged me. I crossed the foyer behind Marco, guided by Brian's flashlight. I could feel Barrios's breath on my neck. I hadn't remembered the layout of the house before, but now that I was inside, it came back to me.

I wiped blood from my lips and chin. The dazzling pain was over, but there was an awful throbbing, and my nose seemed to be growing in size.

The bedrooms were in the wing of the house that faced the swimming pool and the tennis court. There were three of them. Each had its own bath. The master bath was, I recalled, an oversize affair with two wash basins, a sunken tub and a separate shower stall. I wondered whether that was the room Brian had entered and whether Schroeder had noticed the broken window.

Brian led us across the family room. He kept the light away from the sliding door, but even so I noticed that it was open slightly. Was this how Schroeder had got into the house? I doubted it. He probably had a key, stolen by Barrios.

We entered a corridor. Brian turned into the first doorway on the right. The master bedroom. Brian paused to play the light in all directions. It lingered over a stain on the carpet. That, I guessed, was where Blanche Petacque had fallen. An oversized dressing table ran half the length of one wall. It was covered with an array of perfume bottles. And, in front of the perfume bottles, I saw a hairbrush. A large one. It appeared to be heavy. I longed to reach for it.

"This way," Brian said sharply. "The tub."

Schroeder came into the room with the other flashlight.

The tub, I thought. A sunken tub.

Brian moved toward the bathroom. Marco followed him. I followed Marco. Schroeder got between us.

"Not the bathroom," I said. "The dressing table."

Schroeder hesitated. I took his place behind Marco. We entered the bathroom, Brian first, then Marco, then I. I turned sideways, keeping Barrios out.

Brian beamed the flashlight along the wall over the wash basins, at the frosted-glass door of the shower stall, and finally at the window over the tub. "My God!" he shouted. "Somebody's broken the window!"

Marco's head turned.

Brian swung the flashlight.

Barrios moved his gun in Brian's direction. I grabbed his wrist with both hands and pulled.

Brian's flashlight caught Marco on the right temple. Marco staggered toward the tub.

Barrios fired. Glass shattered. I hung onto his wrist, pulled again and extended my foot. He fell against one of the wash basins.

Brian swung, again. Marco went over the edge of the tub, dropping his gun and grabbing at air.

Schroeder tried to squeeze into the room, but he couldn't get past Barrios and me.

Barrios fired again. Something stung my left arm.

Schroeder lashed out at me with his fist, but didn't connect.

I forced Barrios's gun hand into the wash basin and held it there. Brian jammed it against a spigot. Barrios jerked convulsively. But he released the gun. I pulled him toward the tub.

Brian picked up the gun and fired it. Barrios screamed and fell against me.

I felt myself slipping.

I had an instant of great pain. Then everything went black.

– 42 –

The Saturday I left the hospital it rained. And rained hard.

Carol drove. I sat beside her, my seat belt tight, my feet braced against the floorboard, one hand gripping the door handle, nervous as hell. "Take it easy," I kept saying, "watch out for that car, slow down, we're coming to a light."

"Don't worry," she kept telling me, "I see it, we're only doing thirty, relax."

Carol isn't the best driver in the world, however, and I couldn't relax. I'd experienced a great deal of pain during the past two weeks and wasn't anxious for any more. In addition to a broken nose and a severe concussion, I'd been treated for a bullet wound in my left arm, a fractured shoulder and multiple lacerations on my back, one of which had required sixteen stitches.

I'd learned many things during my stay in Phoenix. But the lesson I'd remember longest, it seemed to me, was never to go near a sunken bathtub. Especially one that is littered with shards of glass.

I was luckier than Marco, however. He'd suffered a fractured skull and been unconscious for nine days. And Barrios was still in the hospital too. The bullet Brian had fired at him had ruptured his spleen. The doctors still didn't know whether he'd pull through.

Brian, of course, was the hero of the affair. He'd not only shot Barrios, he'd also captured Schroeder. Tackled him in the bedroom, pistol-whipped him, locked him in a closet and calmly called the police. Close as Brian and I had become, I had to admit that I really didn't understand him. He was handling his notoriety with a shyness and modesty that was very becoming. Yet there was a streak of ruthlessness in him that couldn't be denied. He'd described his fight with Schroeder to me in an offhand way as if it had been nothing at all, a mere tussle, but I'd perceived that it had been considerably more than that and I'd remarked that he must have hurt Schroeder rather badly. At which point his smile faded a hard glint came into his eyes, and he said, "I wish I'd killed the son of a bitch." And there was no doubt that he meant it.

The trip from St. Luke's Hospital to the motel shouldn't have taken more than fifteen minutes, but with the rain, my constant admonitions, and Carol's lack of familiarity with the area, it took almost three-quarters of an hour. Carol parked the car alongside the wing of the building where my room was located, and we hurried through the rain to the passageway that led to the stairs. Or rather she hurried and I did my best to keep up with her—I was still sore in a number of places. When we reached the passageway, I paused for a moment. I don't know what prompted me to do so. Perhaps it was remembered fear. I felt for a moment Barrios's arm closing around my throat, I felt the gun at my back, I even heard the voice—"You come." I shuddered.

"What's the matter?" Carol asked.

"Nothing," I said.

We climbed the steps and walked along the corridor to my room, which Carol had been occupying for the past ten days, ever since her unannounced arrival, with Mark, at my hospital bedside. She unlocked the door.

Everyone shouted, "Surprise!"

I just stood there. The room had been decorated with paper streamers, a "WELCOME HOME" sign had been Scotch-taped to the mirror over the dresser, and there were several bottles of champagne on the desk. "Well, I'll be damned!" I said finally. The last thing in the world I wanted that afternoon was a party.

But as it happened, I enjoyed myself. There were six of us: Ed, Daisy, Brian, a girl I'd never seen before, Carol and myself. The girl I'd never seen before was Millicent Harvey. Brian had mentioned that he'd been spending time with her, and I was pleased to make her acquaintance. She was a pretty little brunette and she was obviously very much attracted to Brian.

Daisy still looked peaked. She'd had a very bad time. She'd been drugged and bound and abandoned in a shack some twenty miles northeast of Phoenix, near the town of Carefree. The shack was on a twelve-acre tract that Schroeder had purchased as an investment for Mutual Claims and then hadn't been able to unload. Since Schroeder had insisted he didn't know her whereabouts, she hadn't been rescued until the day after Barrios came out of surgery, when he made a full confession. By then the drug had worn off, but she was suffering from dehydration. She too had been to see me in the hospital, however. And she was visiting Tom every day.

For Dr. Champion had found that Tom was indeed suffering from acute anxiety and had recommended that he be hospitalized for at least a month. Daisy had arranged to have him transferred from Arizona State Hospital to Camelback Hospital, where Champion was on the staff, and he was improving rapidly. But he hadn't yet reached the point where he could be brought up to date on everything that had happened. All he knew was that

Schroeder had been arrested, Jackley was under investigation, and his father and sister had gone home.

I drank two glasses of champagne and ate some chocolate chip cookies. Millicent had baked the cookies herself and was proud of them, which she had a right to be—they were good. I told her what people always tell pretty girls who bake cookies: that she'd make some man a good wife. And I gave Brian a significant glance. He blushed.

Millicent smiled. "Brian's a lovely teddy bear," she said, "but I'm afraid he might bite." Which showed that Millicent was no fool.

Ed reported that he'd been horseback riding early that morning, and we talked for a while about horses and rain and mountain trails. We also talked about the garment industry, which was very much on Carol's mind, since her boss had been calling her every day to come back to work. And about a French restaurant called Etienne's, which Ed had taken Daisy to the night before.

No one mentioned Schroeder or Mutual Claims or Jackley, Smith.

At four o'clock Carol decided that I should rest. Ed and Daisy left, taking Millicent with them. Carol began to pull down the paper streamers. Brian poured himself another glass of champagne. I tried to help Carol, but it hurt when I lifted my arm so I too poured myself some champagne, took my shoes off and made myself comfortable. I raised my glass to Brian and said, "Teddy bear."

He grinned, then became serious. "I forgot to tell you," he said. "Mr. Price called again last night." Mark had been calling daily, ever since his return to New York. Sometimes twice a day—once to talk to me, once to talk to Brian.

"What did he have to say?" I asked.

"He thinks Mutual Claims has finally stabilized." The price of the stock had dropped forty-six points in the two weeks since Schroeder's arrest.

"For the time being," I said. It would drop a lot more when all the facts came out. So far Schroeder had been charged with conspiracy to commit murder and with kidnapping, but not with fraud. The investigation into the company would take months. I'd done what I could from my hospital room to help the men from the Justice Department, and Brian had been cooperating with them too, but none of us really knew what Mutual Claims had actually been earning. It was beginning to appear, however, that for the first two years of its operation the profits had been what the annual report said they were. But after that Schroeder had begun making bad investments and trying to cover them up. Furthermore, in his eagerness to promote growth he'd been underselling his competitors to such an extent that Mutual Claims was actually losing money on many of the hospitals it was servicing. "Eventually it will drop a lot more," I told Brian.

"The SEC has also started an investigation," he said. "They're investigating us, along with Mutual Claims."

I sighed. The SEC would give us a hard time. But in the end we'd be cleared. We'd done nothing wrong. "Have you talked to anyone at INS?" I asked.

Brian nodded. "So far, nothing." The two wetbacks who'd helped Barrios and Marco were named Garcia and Alvarez. They'd got away. The Immigration and Naturalization Service investigators were still looking for them.

Carol removed the "WELCOME HOME" sign from the mirror. She turned to me. "You're not resting," she said reproachfully.

"Yes, I am," I told her. "Champagne is very restful."

"You're talking business. You shouldn't be talking business."

"What's wrong with talking business?"

"It's not good for you."

"Have you a better idea?"

She thought for a moment. Then she smiled. "Let's play a game. You be the patient, and I'll be the nurse."

"That lets me out," Brian said. He put his glass down, went into the adjoining room and closed the door.

And Carol and I played patient and nurse.

When properly played, it's a great game.